CW01429749

I'm not

USELESS

I am ...

Onesimus

A fictional novel based on Paul's letter to Philemon

... includes ...

Contemplations for Individual Reflection and

Group Discussion

© Copyright: Gary B Lewis 2025

All rights reserved. No part of this publication may be reproduced, stored in a retrieval system or transmitted in any form by any means, electronic, mechanical, photocopying, recording or otherwise, without the prior permission of the publisher / author.

Layout and design by Gary B Lewis

Cover picture © Canva - digitally modified. Used with permission

Lewis, Gary B, 1952—

I'm not Useless: *I am Onesimus*

1. Christian—Fiction. 2. Faith—Personal I. Title.

ISBN: 978-0-6455552-9-5

Scriptures identified as ESV © 2007, 2011, 2016, 2025. Used with permission

Scriptures identified as NIV © 1973, 1978, 1984, 2011. Used with permission

Scriptures identified as NLT © 2004, 2007, 2013, 2015. Used with permission

Paul's Letter to Philemon adapted from EasyEnglish Bible Copyright © MissionAssist 2019 - Charitable Incorporated Organisation 1162807. Used by permission.

Song: Who You Say © Hillsong. Used with permission

Song: He Paid a Debt: Author unknown

PUBLISHED BY GARY B LEWIS

Cranbourne East, VICTORIA 3977

www.gablesbooks.com

DISCLAIMER / TRIGGER WARNING:

The content of this book may be deeply disturbing or emotionally distressing for some readers, especially in the first half. It includes explicit and sensitive material such as verbal abuse, dominance, sexual behaviours ranging from unwanted attention to assault, betrayal, manipulation, anger, and thoughts of suicide and murder.

If you find yourself emotionally impacted by these themes, the author encourages you to seek professional support or counseling.

TABLE OF CONTENTS

ACKNOWLEDGEMENTS

This book is dedicated to the following men who have mentored me over the past fifty-plus years. Some have influenced me from a distance through audio recordings and videos, some through their books, and others through face-to-face conversations.

Rex Beech, Ken Gardiner, Dr. Reg Klimionok, Dr. Robert Schuller, Zig Ziglar, and Rev. John Evans.

Each one of them has helped me not only to discover my full potential and giftings by recognising that I am not useless, but rather a new creation in Christ.

Above all, I thank the Lord Jesus Christ, who loved me and gave His life for me. 'I'm chosen, not forsaken. I am a child of God.' (Hillsong)

And for that reason, I have chosen to 'become a meaningful specific... not a wandering generality.' (Zig Ziglar)

PROLOGUE

*H*ave you ever read the Apostle Paul's short letter to his friend Philemon in the New Testament? If not, I encourage you to go and read it now before doing anything else.

Oh, you have read it? Great. Well, go back and read it again anyway — it's a very short letter after all.

I'll wait here …

Okay, you're back already! What did you make of it?

Most people respond with comments like: "Powerful … personal … persuasive." But dig a little deeper, and you might hear thoughts like: "I have no idea who Philemon is, (pronounced either '*Fie-lee-mon*' or '*Phil-ah-mon*') apart from the fact that a church met in his house." Or: "Onesimus — how do you even say that? One-see-mus? Oh-nes-ee-mus?" "Who was he? A slave? What did he do?" "What was he doing in Rome, anyway?"

Bible scholars often refer to the book of Acts and Paul's other epistles to gather some answers about these two figures. Yet most of them can only speculate about further details — where they lived, when exactly they lived, and how they were first connected to Paul.

Is speculation just a cop-out to avoid saying, "We simply don't know"? Or is it a way of staying close to the available text without making unfounded claims?

I'll be upfront — I am not a Bible scholar, though I love studying scripture. Nor am I a historian, though I am fascinated by history.

When I read scripture and history, I see many stand-alone moments and individuals — like dots on a chart — that stick out ... yet remain disconnected. As a writer, I cannot help but try to connect those dots!

Oh yes! And if you enjoy a good play on words — after all, that's what makes a really good joke or anecdote — then you'll love this one: *"I'm not useless... I am Onesimus."*

If you've read my previous book, *He Took My Lunch*, you'll understand where I'm coming from. If not, you're missing out on some incredible possible connections between three of Jesus' most wonderful miracles.

So, as with my previous book, here's my disclaimer:

If you're a biblical conservative traditionalist — someone who insists on sticking strictly to the text — you may find your understanding challenged. I can almost hear you saying, "If it's not in the text, we don't need to know!" So prepare yourself. You may feel compelled to think beyond a rigid "stick to the text" mindset. And, at some point, you might even be tempted to call me a heretic!

To be honest, the first part of this book is fairly dark. Writing it, took me far outside my comfort zone. Keep in mind though, that we *are* painting a picture. The second half of the story shifts toward my preferred style — where light begins to shine, colours emerge, and contrasts come into focus.

At first, I hadn't planned on including any reflective questions. But after writing the first chapter, I felt compelled to add some — either for personal reflection or group discussion. Since the first half of this book is rather weighty, these questions will offer space for your heart and mind to process what you've read.

As I wrote this book, I found myself constantly referring to my sketchy time-frame — albeit speculative. Having tidied it up, I decided to include this at the back of the book for the benefit of those readers who also need a time-frame checker.

Oh ... one more thing! I hope that by the end of this book, you will be able to identify with Onesimus in some small way.

CHAPTER ONE

USELESS BOY

Circa AD 40

*K*yrios (Master) Phil often observed from a distance, watching the young doulas (slave) boy fumbling about — completely unaware of where he was or what he was supposed to be doing. Despite Onny's cheerful demeanour, he always seemed to the Kyrios to be chasing after a goal he couldn't grasp — like he was the goose in a wild goose chase. The Kyrios would grunt cynically and mutter to himself, "Useless boy! Totally useless!"

Onny was an awkward lad: clumsy, bungling, and all fingers and thumbs. Yet, he wasn't lazy. Always respectful to the Kyrios, he was eager to please and keen to help. Unfortunately, Onny lacked proactive thinking — a sharp contrast to his older wendme (brother), Aegie. Unlike Onny, Aegie was dexterous, competent, and always thinking ahead. He looked out for Onny, often shielding him and guiding him through their duties.

Aegie, a few years older than Onny, had matured quickly under the weight of their shared responsibilities. He worked hard to keep his little brother focused, knowing the Kyrios' watchful eyes were always a potential threat. While Onny relied heavily on Aegie's guidance, there were times he had to handle simple tasks alone — like tending the chicken yard. Whether collecting eggs, feeding the chickens, or cleaning, Onny never knew where to start.

He would often gather eggs, set them in a corner, and then step on them while sweeping. Other times, he'd throw food scraps to the chickens, only to sweep up the area before they'd had a chance to eat. On occasion, he'd forget to bring the basket for eggs, carrying them precariously in his arms, only to stumble and break several. If he wasn't dropping eggs, he was tripping over chickens.

Aegie respected Kyrios Phil and dutifully obeyed his orders. He made sure Onny stayed close by his side, both to learn the ropes and to keep him out of trouble. The boys, being of African heritage, had distinct appearances — although Aegie's skin was much darker than Onny's. Aegie had tight curly black hair, whereas Onny's hair was less curly and blackish-brown.

Their parents, were childless when purchased by Kyrios Dolion brought to his Laodicean estate as douloi (slaves). Unbeknown to Dolion however, the woman was pregnant at the time. Dolion had treated the North African couple quite favourably, but as was customary, any children born to slaves also became the Kyrios' property.

Tragedy struck when the boys' mother died from childbirth complications with her third child, a baby girl who didn't survive. Onny was six; Aegie was ten. Shortly after the death of his wife their father, Ktakyie, overcome with grief; sank into depression and struggled to fulfill his duties. His sons, though grieving themselves, stepped up, taking on extra chores to cover for him.

One morning, Onny awoke to find Aegie sobbing beside their father's bed. Behind him stood the young Kyrios Phil, looking rather indifferent. Aegie turned to his brother and said, "Onny, our Abaye died during the night." Overwhelmed with emotion, the young boy flung himself onto his father's body, wailing uncontrollably. Aegie held his brother tightly, drawing him back whilst trying to console him and whispering, "Our Kyrios Phil will send some men to remove Abaye's body soon." [After his father Dolion's passing, Phil had inherited the property, including all the servants and slaves.]

Phil tentatively placed a hand on Aegie's shoulder, dispassionately offering his condolences. It had been a long time since he'd had any physical contact with the slave boy. "Your father probably died of a broken heart," he said matter-of-factly. As he turned to leave, he added coldly, "After the burial, it will be back to work. Understand?"

"Yes, Kyrios Phil," Aegie replied, whilst covering Onny's mouth to stifle his protests. Before leaving, Phil callously added, "And by the way, you can drop the 'Kyrios Phil.' From now on, it's just 'Kyrios.' Understand?" Aegie nodded. "Yes, Kyrios."

Once Phil had left, Onny sobbed, "Where will they take Abaye? Will they bury him next to Emaye?" Aegie wiped away the tears from their eyes and reassured him, "Yes, Onny. I'm sure they will do what's right."

"But what will happen to us now?" Onny cried. "I'm frightened Aegie. Who will take care of us? What will we do without Emaye *and* Abaye?"

Aegie pushed his own grief aside to comfort his brother. "I will look after you, Onny. You must stay close to me and do what the Kyrios says. We are blessed to have food, a roof, and a bed. We'll be okay," he said reassuringly.

"And … we have work?!" Onny interjected with a smile.

"Yes, as slaves we'll always have work. But we'll manage."

Onny nodded seriously. "And we mustn't call him 'Master Phil' anymore, right? Just Master."

"That's right," Aegie replied. "When it's just between us, we can say 'Kyrios Phil', but when we talk to him, we will only address him as 'Kyrios'".

The brothers hugged in silence until strangers arrived to take their father's body. They pushed the boys out of the way. They roughly manhandled the body without any sense of dignity. "Can we come with you, please?" Onny begged.

Their cold-hearted response unnerved Onny even more. "No!" one of the men snapped. "The Kyrios said for us only to show you the burial site later."

As they departed, Onny burst into tears once more, feeling voiceless, powerless and useless — a weight he would carry for years to come — after all, he was a slave.

❧

CHAPTER TWO

MORE THAN EXPECTED

Circa AD 29-30

*K*yrios (Master) Dolion acquired two young douloi (slaves) — Ktakyie and his wife, Zuhrah who were from North Africa. He had spotted them when he was passing through the slave market in the ancient Galatian capital city, Ancyra. He had no intention or need for buying any slaves at this particular time, but these two douloi had stood out amongst the other slaves up for sale — firstly because they were much younger and despite their slender build, they looked fit, agile and strong; and secondly because the sign next to them which read: 'FOR SALE: Husband and Wife — will not separate!' It seemed strange to him that other traders showed very little interest in acquiring them.

"They'll do!" he said to himself rather smugly. "I'm certain that they'll be productive in more ways than one!" He could envisage them working on his large estate in the city of Laodicea, in the Asian region of Phrygia.

Laodicea had been founded as an active and commercially aggressive competitor to Colossae. Within in a very short time, Laodicea had become famous for its trade, banking, medicine, and textiles. With the establishing of Laodicea and nearby Hierapolis, Colossae's importance as a business centre had diminished significantly around one hundred and fifty years earlier.

Unfortunately though, both Colossae and Laodicea, along with neighbouring Hierapolis, had been severely damaged by earthquakes during the reign of Tiberius (AD17), and again more recently during the reign of Nero (AD60). Many businesses and private property owners suffered greatly, but somehow, Dolion's investments and property incurred only minor damage.

The family's main business interest had been in textiles for generations, which Dolion had inherited from his father. Dolion's father envisaged an opportunity to relocate from the struggling Colossae some fifty years previous, resulting in him successfully establishing his textile business in Laodicea. Dolion's inheritance of the business was a natural process with his father's passing. Their textile manufacture and trade was renowned for its quality fabric including the manufacture of a beautiful dark red wool cloth (*colossinum*).

Dolion had never purchased a slave couple before, and so he was very eager to put them to work on his large Laodicean estate. Their daily tasks combined would involve anything from woodcutting, digging, planting, carrying water, emptying toilet pans, cleaning floors and washing clothes, harvesting as well as tending livestock and poultry. Ktakyie and Zuhrah adjusted to their new working regime well — which pleased the Kyrios Dolion very much. In fact, Ktakyie proved to be such a diligent worker, that the Kyrios allocated him extra duties involving the monitoring of stock and textile quality control.

They were both keen to establish themselves as industrious workers, and because they were purchased as a married couple, the Kyrios granted them a special favour — they were permitted to have their own private accommodation in a lean-to (stoa) beside the main work-shed, away from the shared lodging of the other dozen or so slaves and servants.

After a few months, the talk around the estate amongst the servants and other douloi (slaves), was that Zuhrah was pregnant. By the time news had reached the Kyrios Dolion, it was very clear to him that there was no doubt that in fact she would have been at least a couple of months pregnant at the time when they were traded for a good sum.

Being a pregnant doulos, however, did not excuse her from carrying out her assigned tasks — mainly involving house cleaning, washing clothes and food preparation. However, once the Kyrios was informed of Zuhrah's pregnancy, he seemed intrigued. Thus he developed a special interest in her, and quietly gave instructions for her duties to be lightened, especially as her time for delivery approached.

When the time came for the delivery of her baby, she was assisted by a local maieutikos (mid-wife). As was the custom from where she came from, after a days' rest, she returned to her work duties, carrying her infant boy wrapped in a baby wrap on her back — a very natural way for a mother to keep her baby safe and to form a strong bond. It was a traditional and convenient way which made it possible for her to keep her hands free to continue working, cooking, cleaning, and doing everyday tasks.

Another favourable gesture the Kyrios Dolion granted them was permission for Ktakyie and Zuhrah to name their first born son, as they chose. He did this on the basis that she was already 'with child' when he purchased them. They decided to name their tiny dark-skinned baby boy Aegeus — when means 'protector.'

As her pregnancy progressed however, the forty-year-old Kyrios Dolion, also began taking more notice of Zuhrah. Dolion observed that her already beautiful brown complexion became even more radiant, shining like the glow of brown gold. Her tight jet-black hair glistened brightly in the sunlight, as her shapely body took an extra layer of beauty and elegance. Every day he would position himself on his veranda or balcony to sit and gaze upon her seductive beauty. Day after day, he began to sensually fantasise about being with this stunningly beautiful slave woman.

He somehow managed to restrain his self-indulgent desires, knowing he already had a healthy sexual relationship with his wife, despite having only one child, Philemon. Dolion had often thought it would have been good for his son to have a brother to play with, even though Philemon was already ten years old by this time.

Dolion's gawking behaviour and fantasies did not diminish however, even after Zuhrah gave birth to Aegeus. If anything, they only escalated as he watched her nursing and caring for the baby. In time Dolion also drew much pleasure in watching little Aegeus learning to run about and exploring the world of nature for himself.

As time went on, both Dolion and his wife Nikolette loved watching their own son, taking this little toddler under his wing. They could tell that he really enjoyed having a little friend to play with ... even though he *was* a Black Doulos.

The young master gave his little friend the nickname ... Aegie. And as Aegie found it hard to pronounce Philemon, his older friend suggested that he just call him ... Phil.

Phil obviously loved teaching Aegie things about flowers and trees, insects and birds, bouncing flat stones on the lake, and teaching him words in the Greek and Roman dialects.

Gradually Nikolette grew increasingly uneasy as she noticed Dolion seemed overly focused on Aegie's mother. She observed him ogling Zuhrah, which both offended and embarrassed her as she speculated on his thoughts. In response, Nikolette began to distance herself from him — conversationally, emotionally, and intimately — as a form of punishment.

I'M NOT USELESS ...

Deprived of his husbandry privilege of marital intimacy, Dolion found his desires growing stronger, further intensifying his lustful feelings toward Zuhrah.

≪∾

Contemplations for Individual Reflection and Group Discussion

CHAPTER #1:

- Have you ever been called useless or a klutz? (Or some other derogatory term?) How did it make you feel? How did you handle it?
- What levels or degrees of grief can you identify in the first chapter?
- Describe the brothers' relationship from both angles.
- What are your thoughts on the stark contrast between the senior Master Dolion and the young Master Phil?

CHAPTER #2:

- Think about a time when you have had to do menial tasks for someone else. How did you feel? What did you learn?
- Have ever been shown special favour by an employer?
- Have you ever watched someone ogling at another person, or have you experienced being aware of someone ogling at you? How did it make you feel?
- What do you think of a spouse/partner withholding sex as a form of punishment?

CHAPTER THREE

A MASTER PLAN

Circa AD 33

*A*s time when on, Dolion decided it was time he came up with a plan. He determined to devise a scheme by which he would lure Zuhrah into his bed. He had ogled long enough, and since his wife had withdrawn herself from him, he needed to take matters into his own hands.

It dawned upon him in the early hours one morning late in Spring, that he would write a letter to his wife's cousin, Claudia in Ephesus. Even though he did not really like Nikolette's cousin at all, he was very politely ingenious in writing his letter. He explained how his wife, has been under considerable stress of late, and that he was thinking it would to beneficial for her wellbeing if she was able to get away for a while — and have a holiday by the sea.

He warmly suggested that she might consider inviting Nikolette to spend some time with her, as he proposed how much she would benefit from spending time with her beloved cousin and her daughter, Apphia. He also subtly requested that Claudia not say anything to Nikolette about his request in her reply.

Once it was written and sealed with his personal waxen seal, the letter was promptly sent via his courier-servant. The courier was given strict instructions to wait for Claudia's handwritten reply, before returning home.

Claudia's written letter of reply was warm and inviting. She was careful not to indicate that Dolion had made any contact with her whatsoever.

"Claudia, cousin of Nikolette.

To my dearest cousin Nikolette, wife of Dolion and mother of Philemon. Greetings to you, my dear one. It has been way too long since we last spent time together. You have been so much on my mind lately, so I decided to write to you and invite you to come and spend some time with me and your niece Apphia.

PS — please bring Philemon with you so that Apphia and he can get to know each other better. It won't be too many more years and they can get married!

Please give my regards to Dolion."

Dolion reclined on his portico, wine in hand, gazing out over the tranquil garden courtyard. A satisfied smile played on his lips; the first stage of his scheme now set in motion. The next step loomed ahead — what to do with the husband slave?

His thoughts drifted through various possibilities, each scenario aimed at keeping the husband slave occupied for at least a week, thus granting him unfettered access to the slave woman. And then there was the matter of their young son, Aegeus. That, too, required a clever twist in his master plan.

As he pondered the options, one particular idea began to crystallize, standing out from the rest like a stroke of brilliance.

֍

Chapter Four

THE PLAN UNFOLDS

*F*arewells are never easy — except in this case. Dolion kissed his wife and son goodbye as they climbed into their carriage, which would take them to Ephesus. He stood in the gateway, waving and pretending to appear forlorn, but inwardly, his secret passionate infatuation began to intensify immediately.

As soon as they were offsite and on their way, he summoned Ktakyie to his office and told him to prepare for a journey the following day. There were some business transactions which needed urgent attention ... such as visiting various business owners who specialised in certain coloured dyes — he was to check out if there were any new dyes available on the market — especially purple.

A doulos was never to question their Kyrios under any circumstance, yet Ktakyie had just done so, putting his life at risk. With his head still bowed, he spoke: "Yes, Kyrios. I understand ... but ... if I may ..." he gulped, before being dismissed."

"Well then, what is it doulos?" demanded Dolion.

"Kyrios, if I may make an observation ..." Ktakyie began nervously.

"Well, get on with it then will you? I haven't got all day to stand and chatter with every slave that comes in here!"

"Master, with respect, I believe we already have a good supply of dyes."

"Yes, I know that Ktakyie!" declared Dolion raising his voice vexatiously. "Planning ahead is an extremely important component in my business affairs. One never knows what's around the corner."

He paused briefly to catch his breath, then spoke in a more tolerant manner. "And by the way, you've taken a great risk in questioning my judgment, for which I am willing to overlook on this occasion, as this business matter cannot be delayed any longer."

"Yes, Kyrios. Thank you" replied Ktakyie.

"Oh ... and one more thing. It would be beneficial for you to take your son along with you. It will be a good learning experience for him. I will arrange for horses, supplies for your journey, including your leave-of-absence documents, letters of introduction, and money for any purchases. That is all. Now go!"
"Yes, Kyrios. Thank you." Ktakyie kept his eyes lowered and his head bowed as he backed out of the room.

∽

The next morning just after sunrise, Ktakyie and Aegie set off with two horses and a pony for Aegie. He was very excited about going on his first trip with his Abaye and his first official ride on a pony.

Dolion settled down for his after-breakfast-drink of wine. He was feeling rather pleased with himself, now that part two of his scheme had been actioned. It was time for part three — the *kommáti antístasis* (pièce de résistance) — the cherry on the top of his cake! He had envisioned this final stage for so long, and now adrenaline was beginning to surge throughout his body.

About three o'clock in the afternoon, most people would normally have about an hour of rest. So he sent word through one of his servant girls to find Zuhrah. His instructions were to bring him a cup of wine to his bedroom chamber.

When she arrived, with the chalice in hand, Dolion was already reclining on the bed. He motioned for her to enter and place the chalice on the bedside table. As she did so, he softly said "Thank you." Quickly he reached out and grabbed hold of her arm — firmly but gently. "Please wait and stand there so I can look at you."

A rush of fear flooded over her. What did he have in mind? She knew well that the risk of refusing an order from the Kyrios could be fatal.

The next few moments for her seemed like an eternity of shame and pain. He very gently but firmly overpowered her petite form. She felt completely numb.

Zuhrah scrambled to dress herself after the Kyrios had accomplished what he'd intended all along. She shuddered before she left, as Dolion instructed her to come back at the same time tomorrow. She raced out of the house trembling with disgust, shame and fear.

With each passing day, she became more tense and desensitized. By the end of the week, she began to resist, which caused the master to become quite agitated and gradually more forceful with her.

～

Contemplations for Individual Reflection and Group Discussion

CHAPTER #3:

- Have ever experienced someone who has schemed or plotted behind your back? When you found out ... how did you react?
- Have you ever schemed or plotted behind someone else's back? What was your motive in doing so?

CHAPTER #4:

- Have you ever spoken up to a boss ... questioning their instructions? What happened? How did they respond?
- Can your remember your first 'big' adventure as a child?
- Have you ever experienced being taken advantage of ... or have you had someone exercise power over you? What were your feelings?

CHAPTER Five

A TIME TO BE BORN ...

USEFUL

e

Circa AD 33-34

*N*ickolette enjoyed her time away in Ephesus, with her cousin Claudia. Philemon and Apphia also enjoyed their time together on many adventures. It pleased their mothers to know that secretly their children would hopefully get married. Claudia was a widow, doing her best to raise her daughter and provide for them both, through her home craft business, despite the fact that her health was not the best. Nikolette tried to persuade her to come and live with her family in Laodicea, but Claudia was very stubborn.

Upon arriving home, Nikolette noticed that Dolion seemed to be rather tired, irritable and distant — although he perked up on listening to Phil's adventure stories with his cousin. Nikolette had missed her husband, and Phil had missed his little playmate, in Aegie. And so it was, in no time, normal daily routine resumed in the Master's household.

Ktakyie and Aegie arrived home a day later, to find that his wife was cold towards him for the first time in their married life. She did not want to be touched at all, but she softened a bit with Aegie's many hugs. As it had been Aegie's first time away from home, he was full of stories about all that he had seen and experienced ... and the people he'd met along the way. He especially loved being able to ride on the pony. "One day Emaye," he declared, "When I grow up,

26

I want to work with the horses for Kyrios Dolion!" She smiled as she tried to conceal the deep pain in hearing that name.

Despite the trauma she'd endured that week, Zuhrah forced herself to emotionally detach and continue her daily slave duties. Speaking to Ktakyie about what had happened felt impossible — partly because the pain and shame was too great and partly to shield him from anger that might drive him to act rashly.

Over the next few months, it became clear to everyone on the estate that Zuhrah was once again pregnant. Aegie was naturally overjoyed at the thought of having a little brother or sister to play with, and Ktakyie was equally delighted by the news of another child. Yet Zuhrah carried in her heart the burdensome uncertainty of who the child's father might be.

As her pre-natal condition developed, so did her maternal instincts begin to kick in once again. And as her body grew larger, so too she was granted permission to ease back on some of her duties.

For the duration of her pregnancy, Zuhrah had not said anything to her husband about what she had endured during the week he was away several months earlier.

༄

It was customary when a child was born into slavery, that the Kyrios had the absolute right to name the child. And so, when the attending midwife handed Zuhrah her baby boy — this was the same midwife who had delivered Aegie — she commented that this 'this little bundle of boy is perfectly formed and very handsome like his father.'

As he could not be named until the Master had been informed, this yet-to-named baby had much lighter skin than Aegie, his hair was straight, and he had what appeared to be light brown eyes. As Zuhrah nursed her newborn on her breast, she immediately knew who the child's father was ... but what would Ktakyie say? What would his reaction be?

About the same time as the Kyrios was informed of the baby's arrival, Ktakyie arrived and went into the lean-to/stoa. Despite the fact that the light was dim and particles of dust filled the space, he instantly identified the marked differences in this little one — whom he'd thought all along was his. Without saying a word to his wife, he turned and left.

He was confused and angry. Why had his wife kept this secret from him? He was even more angry at the man who would have done this! With adrenaline racing throughout his body, he ran as fast as he could, away from everything and everyone.

When he eventually stopped to catch his breath, he found himself in the middle of a field of barley. In his furious rage he screamed at the top of his voice, "Why? What now? What am I going to do?"

In the meantime, little Aegie was filled with much joy and excitement to meet his new little brother. "What's his name Emaye?" he asked curiously.

"We have to wait for the Kyrios to give him a name, Aegeus." Even as she spoke the name 'Kyrios', a pang of trepidation pounded her heart.

"But why? Can't you and Abaye name him? He's your baby?"

"One day, Aegeus you will understand why. It won't be long before we will know his name. But in the meantime we can still love him … " she hesitated.

"And cuddle him!" Aegie declared. Holding back her tears of sadness, Zuhrah smiled and nodded as she held both her boys closely in her arms.

Once the Kyrios Dolion had been informed that Zuhrah the black slave woman had given birth to a son, he declared to the servant messenger that the boy should be called Onesimus — which means '*useful*'. He made his decision without having even seen the baby. "After all" he said, "another slave would always be useful!"

Dolion sent word back to Zuhrah informing her of what name had been chosen for her son. She was unsure about the meaning of his name — especially as to what it meant for her. However, Aegeus said that he liked the sound of the name, although he found it difficult to pronounce. He boldly announced, "Emaye, I think I'll just call him 'Onny' ... is that okay?"

"Of course, Aegeus," his mother replied with a chuckle. "You can call him Onny."

Later that day, after all his work duties were completed, and his anger had dissipated, Ktakyie returned home to greet his wife and sons. He held the newborn for the first time, and kissed him on the head, despite knowing that this child was the son of another man. "Onesimus, I am Ktakyie. I will be your father, and you will be my son. You are born of your mother Zuhrah — my wife, and your brother is Aegeus. Welcome to our family."

∽

CHAPTER SIX

CARPE DIEM

*T*he following day Zuhrah was back working her regular slave duties, carrying Onesimus cocooned on her back and stopping in the shade when she could, to nurse him to her breast.

Upon hearing news of the arrival of a newborn slave boy, Dolion's curiosity was piqued. He wondered what the child might look like — would he possess the same charm as Aegie? He also wondered if the child was his own.

As he had done countless times before, Dolion took up his usual position on the portico, choosing to observe from a discreet distance. But, as his gaze swept across the scene, it once again found its way to Zuhrah, igniting a renewed spark of interest that stirred his thoughts.

In no time, word quickly spread like a grassfire around the estate about how different Onny was to his older brother. Even twelve year old junior master Philemon noticed the contrasts — although he thought nothing much of it except that the baby looked cute, as that he was pleased for Onny who now had a little brother to play with. Phil was not really that interested in playing with the baby now that he was a bit older, but he still loved spending time with Aegie.

Zuhrah and Ktakyie never discussed the subject of Onny's paternity — it was if a silent agreement on a taboo subject had been reached, on the understanding that she'd had no choice but to comply with being overpowered. They did continue to love each other however, and in due time, resumed their own sexual relationship.

With rumours spreading of Onny's differences in appearance, Nikolette's suspicions began to increase as she kept her husband under strict scrutiny. Whenever she noticed his ogling eyes shift from the baby ... she quickly made some sort of excuse to distract Dolion's attention. Her method of distraction seemed to work more often than not, and fortunately for her, it appeared that he was totally oblivious as to her motives.

Several months went by, and little by little, Onny's unique features began to develop more distinctly from those of his slave parents and his older brother. Thus providing more fuel in the gossip arena around the estate.

Then by chance, one morning after breakfast, Nikolette and Phil left at short notice to visit some friends in Hierapolis — about nine kilometres away. They travelled via a Roman road through the Lycus valley. Their horse and carriage was being driven by her personal assistant.

On that same morning, as luck would have it, Ktakyie requested permission to leave the estate as he needed to deliver some orders for customers. He also left not long after the others in the opposite direction, on horseback for the nineteen kilometre journey, taking Aegie with him.

Despite the dual realization of opportunity catching Dolion off guard, he quickly sprang into action. He ordered one of the servants to summon Zuhrah and her baby under the pretence of wanting to meet the little fellow in person. Overcome with fear and trepidation, she complied without hesitation.

Cradling her infant on her chest, she tentatively made her way into the house, and was led towards a different chamber — the 'andron'. This room was reserved exclusively for entertaining male guests. The room had three couches, and several tables which could be easily slid under the couches, some artwork and any other necessary paraphernalia.

Dolion was already reclining on one of the couches. As Zuhrah entered the room with her eyes down. Flamboyantly he sat up with his arms wide open, and pretentiously welcomed both mother and child. "Here, let me have a good look at this little man. What a handsome looking boy he is. He's very different to his brother ... isn't he?"

Still with her eyes down, she replied awkwardly, "Yes Kyrios, he is." Dolion held out his hands, waiting for her to pass her baby over to him. Cautiously, she handed the master her infant. He held the baby at arm's length for inspection and very quickly placed him down onto the nearby table.

"Now come here, my girl ..." Taking her by the hand he led her over towards the couch. "Now let me have a look at you."

"But Kyrios ... " she protested. And for the first time she lifted her eyes to make contact with his. "My baby! I'm still nursing him!" She knew well the unwritten law of being a slave: '*refusing is both withholding and disrespectful ... withholding is stealing ... both disrespect and stealing are punishable by death* '. Once again her choice was to either comply or die. But this time her concern was not so much for her own wellbeing, but more so for her baby.

"He'll be fine there. Now come!" demanded Dolion. Zuhrah tried to resist and reach out for her baby, but Dolion reached out, to grab her arm away, and at the same time knocked the baby towards the edge of the table.

Dolion dragged her to the couch and forced himself on her. He was much more forceful with her than he had previously been, knowing that he only had a short window of opportunity to play around with.

Zuhrah struggled beneath her master's weight, and as she attempted to scream, he gagged her with one hand and continued thrusting his body up and down onto her light frame. This was the longest time Onny had been out of his mother's embrace, and the insecurity he must have felt suddenly caused him to become restless. Frantically his legs and arms were moving about, as in his desperation his whimpering turned into ear piercing screeching. At which point, the unthinkable happened. Onny fell off the table.

His head hit the marble floor with a crack ... followed by an agonizing moment of silence, not unlike the stillness before a baby's first cry after birth. The baby squealed in shock and pain, but Zuhrah was rendered useless under the weight of the master. In her powerless state, she struggled even more and began sobbing uncontrollably whilst the baby continued to scream in pain.

Once Dolion had finally accomplished his assault, he rose from his position of physical power to one of verbal dominance. He ordered Zuhrah to leave. 'Get out ... and take your useless, squawking child with you! You're going to regret this day, you worthless slave girl!"

[This was the first time Onny had had the label 'useless' declared over his life. Unfortunately, it would not be the last. This 'curse' would haunt him for many years to come.]

Zuhrah staggered to her feet as she adjusted her attire. She scrambled to gather up her distressed baby in her arms. She raced out of the 'andron' as quickly as she could manage after such an ordeal. Feeling quite disorientated she raced through the house looking for a way out.

At long last she found the exit, but who should she meet but the Master's wife, returning from her trip earlier than expected. Apparently there was flooding in the Lycus Valley, and so they turned back. Zuhrah ran frantically as she brushed past Nikolette who was attempting to block the exit.

Outside the doorway, young Phil had to jump out of the way as Zuhrah burst out onto the portico. He turned and watched her run all the way back to their stoa.

Upon arrival she collapsed onto the straw covered mattress, sobbing and cradling her distressed baby still in shock and pain. She tried to comfort him, as she placed his lips onto her breast and hummed a song from her childhood. Eventually, he calmed down as he began to suckle, and drink himself to sleep.

❧

Contemplations for Individual Reflection and Group Discussion

CHAPTER #5:

- Why do people who have experienced trauma — particularly sexual trauma — take so long to talk about it with someone they trust?
- Have you ever remained silent about some traumatic event in your life?
- Think about a decision that was made by someone else that you had no say in whatsoever — e.g. the naming of a child. How difficult is it / was it to accept what you cannot change?

CHAPTER #6:

- In your family, are there or has there been any 'taboo' subjects?
- What's it like living in a situation with someone who is under a pretence? Flip this: what's it like living under a pretence yourself?
- Can you recall the first time someone declared something over your life that was either good or bad as in a blessing or curse?

CHAPTER SEVEN

CONFRONTING THE PAIN OF TRUTH

*L*ater that day, when Ktakyie arrived home, he expected to see Zuhrah working in the garden. When he asked one of the other slave women, she said that she had seen Zuhrah upset earlier, and running with her squealing baby.

He raced towards their lean-to house, only to find his wife curled up in a foetal position, hugging little Onny. Lowering himself quietly onto the bed, he lay down and with much tenderness embraced her. Her reflex reaction to his gentle touch was to jerk away, but as he held her and softly whispered to her words of reassurance and comfort; she relaxed her body back into his. The baby, Onny was at long last, sleeping peacefully beside her.

In the meantime, Aegie had caught up with Phil, who was teaching him how to play marbles made from clay.

⤙

After resting in her husband's arms for some considerable time, Zuhrah was able to express to her husband what had occurred earlier in the day. Even though it was so painful, she managed to describe in detail not only what the Kyrios had done to her that morning, but also what had happened a year ago, and in doing so, confirmed that the Master was Onny's biological father.

Ktakyie held his wife close to him for some time, then he rose up from the bed in an angry rage. "I need some air!" he snapped as he left their small one-roomed house. Storming outside, he found himself running frantically with no particular destination in mind. He just ran ... and ran ... and ran until he'd reached the boundary marker of the property overlooking the valley. Picking up some rocks, he threw them as far as he could, down the cliff-face. With each rock, he yelled, swore and cursed the man who had done this to his family.

After expending so much anger and energy in running, throwing and cursing, he eventually collapsed on the ground. Breathlessly he lay there as he tried to gather his thoughts.

After some time he stood and began walking home. Having released much of his volcanic anger, his steps quickened as he began plotting murderous thoughts towards the Kyrios.

❧

In the intervening time, Nikolette confronted Dolion about what she suspected had transpired between him and the slave woman. His wife detailed how she'd nearly collided with her as she hurried out of the house, carrying a screaming baby. Nikolette had never been so enraged in her life. Her Greek temperament had reached its breaking point. She ranted and raved, bombarding her husband with one question after another. She demanded the truth — not excuses.

Unlike Ktakyie and Zuhrah's conversation, Nikolette and Dolion argued back and forth with accusations of distractions and neglect. Fiery arrows of blame flew in both directions, as did objects that could be thrown. Their raised voices and smashing noises could be heard from all over the estate.

Outside in the dust and dirt, Phil and Aegie were also aware of the yelling coming from inside the house. As he released another marble to attack Phil's collection, Aegie commented, "Wow! That's a lot of loud words ... and crashing. What are they yelling at each other about Phil? What are they saying?"

Phil explained that his mitéra (mother) must be really upset about something that his patéras (father) had done. "It must be serious; I've never heard them that angry before."

Even as Ktakyie was nearing the house, he could still hear the Master and his wife — fighting and smashing. All of a sudden, the yelling stopped ... then a brief moment of silence, came a blood-curdling scream from the Master's wife. "Dolion! No!" And then the wailing began ... "No! No! No!"

‹ઽ

CHAPTER EIGHT

CHANGE

IN THE WAKE

OF LOSS

*K*takyie stopped in his tracks. He stopped walking as he noticed servants running frantically in and out of the house. His murderous thoughts were suddenly disrupted. As one servant ran out another ran in. "The Master is dead!" one yelled as they hysterically raced about spreading the news.

"Did she kill him?" one asked.

"No! He just dropped dead in front of her," another replied.

Yet another instructed, "We must get things organised for the funeral. Come on you lot ... there's no time to waste ... it's already getting late in the day!"

Upon hearing of the Kyrios's sudden death, Ktakyie looked heavenward and quietly declared, "Surely 'Onyame' — our God has intervened!" He found Aegie and Phil still focused on their marbles. He approached asked Aegie to come home, and respectfully informed his 'new' Kyrios, that his mitéra needed his help in the house. Phil jumped up and raced towards the house, while Ktakyie and Aegie walked hand-in-hand to their small house.

News spread quickly throughout the region of Dolion's sudden death. As was customary in their Greek culture, funeral preparations were set in motion. Maintaining respect was very important to the Greeks, which meant that everyone, including servants and slaves, would come to pay homage at the passing of their Kyrios.

Relatives of the deceased, primarily the women, in Dolion's case, included Nikolette's cousin, Claudia and her daughter Apphia — as well as selected servant women — together prepared the prothesis (laying out of the body). Once the body was washed and anointed with oil, it was then placed on a high bed within the house. After this preparation, the body was laid out for viewing on the second day.

The kinswomen ... led by Nikolette, Claudia and Apphia wrapped in dark robes, stood round the bier (the frame on which the body would be carried to the grave). Being the chief mourner, Nikolette was at the head, and others behind. She led the mourning by chanting dirges, as they were tearing at their hair and clothing, and striking their torsos, particularly their breasts. Other relatives and friends also came to mourn and pay their respects to Dolion.

It was before dawn on the third day after Dolion's death, that the funeral procession *(ekphora)* formed to carry his body from the house to its resting place on the outskirts of the property, to where Dolion's parents were both buried. It was a large gathering of family and friends from far afield.

It was customary that once a deceased had been buried, there would be an official period of thirty days of mourning. Over the next month, the immediate family was obliged to visit Dolion's grave on three specific days: the third, ninth, and thirteenth.

It was particularly noticeable to Nikolette and Claudia during this season of mourning, that Philemon and Apphia spent a lot of time together, and their fondness for each other deepened. Saying goodbye to Claudia and Apphia was, therefore, a very emotional time for Nikolette and Philemon, as a close bond of support and love had developed between the four of them on different levels.

Once the month of mourning had officially been completed, life on the estate slowly returned to a new type of normal — albeit very different. While there was undeniably a deep void that lingered in the wake of Dolion's passing, a nebulous atmosphere of calm slowly descended, settling into place like a soft, inevitable quiet after the chaos and uncertainty, mixed with an anticipation of hope.

ᥒᐧ

Contemplations for Individual Reflection and Group Discussion

CHAPTER #7:

- Revenge is a human trait when you realise that you have been wronged. Is revenge in itself helpful or harmful? Is it right or wrong? What are the alternatives?

CHAPTER #8:

- Every culture has certain traditions or rites when it comes to funerals and burials. Compare your cultural traditions with that of the ancient rituals in this chapter. Are you aware of other cultural funeral / burial traditions.

CHAPTER NINE

ASSUME THE POSITION

Circa AD 34

*O*fficially, young Philemon had assumed the title of Kyrios; however, as a mere teenager, he relied heavily on his mother's wisdom and experience. Her first counsel to him was clear: *"Philemon, you will not legally be able to attain full authority as Kyrios until your eighteenth birthday. Until then, you must serve out your apprenticeship, whilst honing your skills necessary for your future role."*

During this transitional period, Philemon needed to immerse himself in their thriving cloth industry, gaining insight into its subsidiaries and financial operations. Equally vital, was mastering the art of managing both servants and slaves. His initial task was straightforward yet essential: learn the names of everyone in their household and on the estate, and gain understanding of their respective roles and duties.

With the passing of Phil's patéras, and his preparations to 'assume the position' of Kyrios within the next few years, his relationship with Aegie was greatly impacted. While they remained friends in their hearts, yet no longer were they able to spend any time together — except when they occasionally passed by each other for a brief moment. These changes also meant that Aegie now had to get used to calling his friend 'Kyrios' Phil.

During this time of adjustments for everyone, Aegie was able to devote more time to helping his Emaye, and getting to play and teach his little brother. Aegie simply adored his brother's warm and loving nature, despite the reality that he was a slow learner and rather clumsy — to say that Onny was uncoordinated would be an understatement! Almost everything that he touched was met with a crash or smash. He especially required extra help at meal times. There was hardly a meal would go by, when he did not get food everywhere — his clothes — his hair — his face including the surrounding area where he'd been sitting.

Aegie was very patient and quickly learned to read the signs of those times when Onny needed extra assistance. Particularly when he started to crawl and toddle about. Aegie was always there to help Onny — whether it was carrying a small bucket of water, or his personal sanitary needs.

Utilising many of the things he had learned from Phil when he was younger, Aegie proved to be an excellent teacher and with the eyes of a hawk. He could spot in an instant, when there was an awkward clumsy accident about to occur, and although he was not always able to prevent the mishap from happening, at least he was there to reassure Onny, and help him clean up — whatever the mess.

As Onny began learning to speak, it became noticeable to those nearby that he fumbled his words out — eventually this became more pronounced into stuttering. Sometimes Aegie would jump in and try to help him out by saying the correct word without any intent of embarrassing his brother.

Circa AD 37

From time to time, the young apprentice master, would pass by and see Aegie and Onny playing or doing a small task. Phil would acknowledge Aegie in a congenial manner, but then as he passed he'd snigger to himself at the awkwardness of the little brother. As he walked on, he'd often turn around and admire Aegie's patience.

Time — as the saying goes — is a healer of many things, but not so in Onny's case. His clumsiness became more pronounced, and as his vocabulary increased so did his stuttering. Ktakyie and Zuhrah discussed their concerns from time to time. Ktakyie had thought it could have been an ongoing consequence of the curse declared over Onny, the day Kyrios Dolion died after abusing Zuhrah. Ktakyie had also entertained the thought that perhaps Onyame (God) was punishing him for his murderous thoughts towards Dolion.

One night in bed, as they quietly discussed Onny's challenges, Zuhrah suddenly recalled the day Dolion raped her — Onny had fallen, hitting his head on the marble floor.

It was a moment of illumination to have a practical answer, besides the speculation of being cursed. It brought both parents a sense of peace and understanding, which helped them develop an even deeper love for both their boys.

Over the next few years, Ktakyie and Zuhrah consistently worked hard at raising their boys to be respectful and helpful, and to each take responsibility for their juvenile slave duties.

∾

In the intervening time, the young master Phil was fast approaching the end of his apprenticeship. But within his heart he was becoming increasingly concerned as to the stark difference between the two slave brothers. Even more bothersome were the noticeable similarities between young Onny and himself.

On one occasion, his curiosity was piqued when he overheard Aegie say to his brother as he was trying to do something, "Onny, you looked just like Kyrios Phil when you did that!" Fortunately, neither Aegie nor Onny had any idea, at that time, what this statement could possibly mean.

It was that comment that prompted Phil, from then on, to observe Onny's expressions and facial features more closely.

Eventually, he could no longer silence his thoughts and so went to confront his mitéra.

It came as no surprise to Nikolette, that her son would raise this controversial topic ... in fact she'd been waiting for him to bring it up for some time. She explained how his patéras had taken advantage of Aegie's mother, while they had been visiting with Claudia and Apphia in Ephesus, causing her to become pregnant.

Phil sat in silence momentarily, then standing to his feet, clenching his fists, and raising his voice, he questioned: "Do you mean to tell me that that useless little so-and-so of a half-cast is actually my brother? No way!"

His mitéra quickly but unemotionally replied, "He's your half-brother Philemon, and he was given his name of 'Onesimus' by your patéras ... without even knowing that he was the father."

"But Mitéra!" he protested, "He's totally useless! Have you seen how clumsy he is? He is completely incapable. And besides he can't even string together one sentence without stuttering! *He is totally* useless!"

Nikolette waited for Philemon's ranting to subside, then with some sense of compassion she said: "My son remember ... this little 'useless' boy you are talking about is only four years old!"

"Maybe ... " retorted Phil, "But I sure hope to the gods that he will grow out of looking like me! Otherwise he will be not only useless ... but an embarrassment as well."

Before he was able to turn and leave, Nikolette spoke assertively yet lovingly. "One more thing Philemon, as you will soon be Kyrios of this estate in your own right, remember this ... you are still my son and I will always be your mitéra. I will always love you just as your patéras loved you. We chose to have you ... you had no say in it. Just like little Onesimus ... he had no say in who his parents would be."

Phil was stunned by his mother's last remarks. He politely excused himself pondering what his new official role might mean for how he treated his half-brother. It certainly would not change the fact that he had a half-brother who was a clumsy-useless-stutterer.

✎

Chapter Ten

Double Grief

~e~

Circa AD 41

*E*ventually, Zuhrah joyfully informed Ktakyie that she was again pregnant. The news brought much excitement to their small family, especially at the thought of perhaps welcoming a baby girl.

Her pregnancy, however, was fraught with difficulties, limiting her to only light duties. The delivery came unexpectedly — about six weeks prematurely. Although premature births were not uncommon, they carried significant risks, particularly for the baby.

From the moment the midwife saw the newborn, she knew something was wrong. The baby girl was blue and lifeless, her neck had been constricted by the umbilical cord. Losing a baby to stillbirth was a heart-wrenching ordeal, but the situation worsened further.

Zuhrah began haemorrhaging heavily. The midwife worked tirelessly to control the bleeding, but soon Zuhrah's body was seized by violent convulsions, as though some unseen force surged through her. After several agonizing minutes, the convulsions stopped, and the bleeding subsided — but tragically, Zuhrah did not survive.

The midwife placed the stillborn baby on Zuhrah's chest, covered them with a sheet, then went to find Ktakyie to deliver the devastating news. Afterward, she went to inform the young master Phil and his mother.

Word of this double tragedy spread quickly, but in contrast to the passing of Dolion, there was no gathering of family or friends to mourn with Ktakyie. This left Aegie and Onny with no one to console them but their father. Their small family, already enduring the bonds of slavery, now faced the unbearable losses of Zuhrah — a beloved wife and mother — and her baby girl.

With guidance from his mother, the new official Kyrios arranged for some male slaves to attend to the wrapping of the bodies in the sheet. They carried them to a pre-dug grave plot on the edge of the property.

Ktakyie and his two sons sombrely followed behind to watch the men place the bodies into the shallow grave. They stood watching in silence for some time as the men shovelled the dirt back over the grave plot. Then as the men left, the wailing began — first Onny, then Aegie and then Ktakyie, who held his sons close.

From that day, Ktakyie seemed to lose all sense of hope. His grief laced with bitterness clawed away at his mind, his will and his strength. As this condition worsened, he even struggled to offer any support or comfort to his grieving boys.

Aegie found this season of mourning particularly difficult, as he not only tried to comfort his little brother, but he also had to step up and take on extra duties to cover for his father who was falling apart at every point.

[NOTE: The further unfolding of this tragic story was told back in chapter one.]

Contemplations for Individual Reflection and Group Discussion

CHAPTER #9:

- Have you ever served an apprenticeship or probationary period in employment? What was it like in that 'on trial - learning' period?
- Sniggering is a form of abuse ... agree or disagree? Have you experienced this as a victim ... perpetrator or bystander?
- Were you ever confronted with the 'truth' about something or someone — when you were too young to fully comprehend all the implications? How did it affect you at the time?

CHAPTER #10:

- Stillbirth is a traumatic loss for parents. Your thoughts / experiences?
- Everyone experiences grief and loss — some more than others. Reflect on you own. How did you cope? What support can you give to others in their grief?

CHAPTER ELEVEN

CHANGES IN

FAMILY LIFE

*Sh*ortly after the official status of Kyrios had been bestowed upon Philemon by his mother, and the whole staff of the estate and local community; word came from Ephesus that Nikolette's cousin Claudia was seriously ill.

Phil quickly took action by ensuring that his mother was safely escorted to Ephesus to visit Claudia, and offer whatever support she could to Apphia in caring for her mother.

Apphia and Nikolette took turns at sitting by Claudia's bedside day-in-day-out, for almost two weeks. It was during this bonding time with her cousin, that Claudia shared with Nikolette, news of a travelling preacher / teacher from Tarsus called Paul. Although she struggled to breathe, she determinedly encouraged Nikolette to find out more. "Some say he's an apóstolos — a sent one — converting Jews, Greeks and Romans to put their faith in the man they call Jesus. He was crucified by the Roman soldiers in Jerusalem. They say he rose from the dead after three days, and ascended before their eyes up to heaven!"

It seemed to both Nikolette and Apphia that Claudia was either delusional or she was speaking in terms of having also put her faith in this Jesus person. To keep her calm, they listened patiently, offering nods of acknowledgment to appease her.

Claudia went on to explain that she had heard stories of Paul's miraculous conversion on the road to Damascus. "He set out with the intent to arrest anyone following this new faith," she said. "But along the way, a blinding light from heaven struck him, leaving him unable to see. Paul was known for his relentless persecution of these followers — driven by a fervent desire to wipe them out. But God seemed to have other plans."

Gasping for breath, she pleaded, "Promise me ... both of you ... that you will seek him out and listen to what he has to say!" With that, she breathed her last.

Despite her sadness at the passing of her dear cousin and best friend, Nikolette was both intrigued and disturbed by Claudia's passing remark. Yet, she had to set those feelings aside to focus on comforting her niece, Apphia.

Together, they and other women who were neighbours prepared the prothesis, after which the body was laid out for viewing on the second day.

The kinswomen ... led by Apphia and Nikolette were the chief mourners. They led the mourning by chanting dirges, tearing at their hair and clothing, and striking their torsos. As there were no other relatives, only friends came to mourn and pay their respects to Claudia. The burial took place just on the outskirts of Ephesus at a designated place reserved for burials.

After the month of mourning rituals, Nikolette assisted Apphia to sell up and pack her belongings. Following Kyrios Philemon's instructions, they travelled back to Laodicea. It had long been agreed that if anything happened to Claudia, Nikolette would take Apphia in as her own daughter.

At twenty-two, Apphia remained unmarried but was at peace with the longstanding arrangement that had betrothed her to her second cousin, Philemon, from an early age.

Within no time, Apphia settled into her new life in the oikos — not just the house itself, but the entire household of servants and slaves. Eventually, Nikolette took on a new role of wedding planner. With Philemon now as the Kyrios, she had to keep him informed of every detail, but she also involved Apphia in the planning as much as possible.

This wedding would require a break in tradition, as Apphia's parents were both deceased, as well as Phil's father; yet despite all this ... the planning proceeded with much joy and anticipation. Having no male figure to give away the bride, it was agreed that with Nikolette legally being the parent-guardian of them both, she would 'give them both away' to each other — and as such no dowry was required. What normally would have been a traditional Greek wedding, would in fact turn out to be very 'nontraditional' in many ways. Thus, the wedding planned was to be much smaller than a traditional wedding.

The celebrations still took place over three days, but many of the usual rituals were either modified or bypassed altogether. Apphia did not have any other relatives on her side of the family, so the guest list consisted of mostly relatives on Philemon's family side as well as friends of the couple.

Phil and Apphie both adjusted well to married life, which in reality, was made easier in many ways, as their love for each other had been deepening over a number of years.

Apphie was keen to learn more about the running of the oikos and the family business. She accompanied Philemon wherever and whenever he would go — whether it was on the estate or to places for business propositions.

She watched as Phil interacted with the servants and slaves — especially when it came to paying their wages. Overall, she observed that he was a fair *Kyrios*, though firm and direct.

Over time, however, she began to notice slight discrepancies in how he dealt with the young slave everyone called Onny. The other slaves received a fixed portion of their *peculium*, but when it came to Onny, Phil would sometimes withhold something — one time a single coin, another time two coins.

As Apphie quietly tracked these deductions, she realized that if this pattern had been happening for some time, then Onny would have been owed a considerable sum.

On one occasion she challenged her husband about her observations. "Phil, why is it that you always underpay that young slave called Onny? That doesn't seem fair to me!"

Phil was indignant, and for the first time ever, they argued. "This is none of your business, Apphie! Just drop it!" With that, he stormed off, leaving her standing there, flabbergasted. His agitation flared into fury in a flash, like when a raw nerve has been jabbed.

Apphie concluded that although she did not understand the underlying reason for her husband short changing Onny, she would not bring it up again. However, she did continue to watch carefully albeit from a distance.

As with any slave or servant interactions with their Kyrios, they always kept their eyes and heads lowered in submission. On one occasion as she stood at a distance, Apphia was startled to see Onny's face for the first time. She had even more questions but who could she ask? She was not willing to risk asking Phil about it at all.

❧

CHAPTER TWELVE

NEW ROLE ...

NEW NAME ...

'A WASTE OF SPACE'

*F*ollowing the deaths of their parents, the two brothers were granted permission by the Kyrios to continue living in their stoa (lean-to house). The stoa had changed very little over the years — it looked just like a covered portico supported by wooden posts. The Kyrios showed them leniency by not forcing them to live with the older slaves. And since he had also been through a time of grief, he also allowed them plenty of time to adjust to do whatever duties they were able to manage.

By staying together, following their double grief, the young slave boys worked even more closely together. Onny especially required guidance and a lot of encouragement handling most of the manual tasks.

As a result of the fall on his head as an infant, Onny remained slow at learning — though he was intelligent. His clumsiness seemed endless, no matter what he attempted. Adding to his struggles, his stutter compounded his already low self-esteem, and what frustrated him most, was his inability to complete a sentence without stammering — no matter how he tried.

Onny would often hear Kyrios Phil mutter as he passed by, "Useless boy! What a waste of space!"

Despite his brother Aegie's constant reassurances, the thought of being useless slowly took root, sinking deeper until it became embedded in his heart and soul. Over time, whenever he fumbled or stuttered, the words would echo in his mind: '*I'm useless! Just as the Kyrios says … I'm a waste of space!*'

❦

As a legacy from his father, Aegie's love for horses continued to develop. It all began with his first pony ride as a four-year-old, and grew stronger each time he accompanied his father on supply trips. By age twelve, he had already gained a reputation for his horsemanship, a skill that naturally extended to breaking in wild horses. To watch him work was a marvel in itself— approaching each animal — it was as if he was able to communicate in a secret language which only the horse and he understood.

As time passed, word of Aegie's equine expertise spread across the district. Eventually, these reports reached Kyrios Phil, and by the time Aegie turned eighteen, he was appointed overseer of the estate's horse stock. His new role put him in charge of housing, feeding, breeding, training, and trading horses. It also placed him in command of other slaves, some twice his age.

Along with this promotion came a new name. In recognition of Aegie's skill and the deep respect Kyrios Phil had held for his father, he bestowed upon him the name *Archippas* — Greek for "Master of Horses." This was not a mere nickname but his new legal identity, officially recorded and stamped with Philemon's waxen seal. A copy was given to Aegie — now Archippas — and another stored securely in Philemon's security safe.

The announcement of his new title and name felt strange to both master and servant. They laughed as Phil said, "I've always called you Aegie, but from now on, I think Archie will suit just fine! What do you say?"

"Thank you, Kyrios Phil. I am deeply honoured," Archie replied, inwardly pleased not only with his new name but with the responsibility it carried.

Eager to share the news, he raced to find Onny. His younger brother's face lit up with excitement.

"You t-t-truly deserve to be c-c-called 'M-M-Master of Horses' — but to me, Aegie, you'll always be 'My p-p-protector!',", Onny said. "Just b-b-between the two of us, I'll s-s-still call you Aegie … if that's ok-k-kay with you."

"Of course, Onny."

෴

Contemplations for Individual Reflection and Group Discussion

CHAPTER #11:

- Can you recall the first time you heard the gospel message of Jesus?
- Have you ever cared for / ministered to / attended to someone in palliative care? What was hard? What was special? What did you learn?
- Have you ever lived with relatives or friends for some time. What were the challenges / benefits?

CHAPTER #12:

- Can you remember when your first discovered a love for animals or a particular interest? What was it that sparked that for you?
- Have you ever been promoted to a new position or given a title? What was that like? How did it affect you?

CHAPTER THIRTEEN

A SHIFT IN

RELATIONSHIPS

Circa AD 55

*I*t was roughly seven years since his promotion and name change, and Archie was now twenty-five years old, when the Kyrios, summoned him to his office chamber in the oikos.

Phil and Aegie had always enjoyed a close friendship despite the fact that it was based on a master-slave relationship. On this particular occasion, the Kyrios sat at his desk with a special looking parchment not unlike the one given when Aegie was given a new name. Next to the parchment was a leather purse.

The Kyrios stood as he picked up the parchment and the purse and extended them towards Archie. "Aegie ... I'm mean Archie ... we have been friends for many years now. I think that it is time that I release you from the friendship we have shared during that time. Now it is time for our friendship to go to a different level. I wish to extend to you your freedom."

Momentarily Archie was speechless, but immediately his thoughts shifted towards his brother Onny. Archie knew how Kyrios Phil felt towards Onny, but he never once held it against him. Archie/Aegie loved his brother very much, and as his name Aegeus meant 'protector', he felt compelled to ask the master what his intentions were for Onny.

"Kyrios, if I may speak" he spoke respectfully, without making eye contact.

"Of course Archie, you will always have a voice in this oikos."

"Thank you Kyrios. I need to know what will happen to my brother. What do you intend for him?"

This interjectory question was somewhat predicted by the master, even though he gave the impression that it caught him off guard. Secretly Phil wished he could sell off Onny to another slave master, but now that Archie had put him on the spot, he pretended to think on his feet and come up with an option that Archie would find difficult to resist.

"Oh yes, about that! Your brother ... he will be kept on here." (He could not even bring himself to use Onny's name knowing full well that it meant 'useful' and the fact that he'd always called him 'useless'). "He will always have a place to stay and will continue to work hard. What do you think Archie?" Although secretly, Phil almost choked on his own words.

"My offer to you as your master and your friend is genuine — meaning that you will be free to go. But you may also consider staying on here as my personal assistant. Neither as a slave nor a servant, but as a friend who gets paid. It would mean that you would have your own sleeping quarters in the house and that your brother could relocate to live with the other slaves. What do you say Archie, my friend? Does this sound like something you would like?"

Again Archie was speechless, as this was more than he would have expected. He stood looking down at the floor for some time, then looking up he spoke respectfully. "Kyrios Phil, I am extremely grateful for your generosity of the freedom you have offered me — which I humbly accept."

The two men looked directly at each other — nodded and smiled. "But to your second offer, on being your personal assistant and Onny's accommodation, I cannot accept ..." He paused briefly. "... without speaking with my brother. After all, he is my only brother, and I am his only family!"

Archie always had his suspicions about his master and his brother being half-brothers. Despite this, it had never once been mentioned between the two of them. It was as if it were an unwritten agreement, never to be exposed or discussed. Aegie was also well aware of how his master despised Onny. This burden of compassionate love was one that Aegie simply had to bear in his complex love-relationship between his brother and his master. Deep within his heart, he hoped that one day he would see them reconciled, but in the meantime, he remained loyal to both.

The Kyrios waited momentarily, not just because Archie's response had taken him by surprise, but also to see if Archie might say something else. "Of course Archie, you take as much time as you need with your brother. I will still be here waiting for your answer."

For the first time in many years, Phil held out his hand as a gesture of true friendship. As they shook hands, their eyes met with a warm intensity.

∽

"B–b–but Aegie! Wha–wha–what will hap–hap–happen to me?" Onny stammered through his protest in response to Aegie's explanation of the Kyrios's offer. "W-w-will we st-st-still be brothers? And who w-w-will wa-wa-watch out f-f-for me, when now y-y-you are f-f-free and living in the K-K-Kyrios's house?"

Aegie / Archie reassured Onny of the master's promise that he would be looked after — even though he would need to live with the other slaves.

"B-b-but Aegie, I'm sc-sc-scared! W-w-we have always slept together in the s-s-same bed. Y-y-you have always b-b-been my pro-pro-protector ... just as your n-n-name means!" He started to tear up as he looked at his older brother.

Aegie placed his hand gently on his brother's shoulder and lifted his head, so he could look him straight in the eye. "Onny, Onny. You will always be my brother — always! And I will always be here for you, especially if any of the other slaves or servants give you trouble. Do you understand? And Onny, I truly believe that one day, Master Phil will also offer you your freedom!

"D-d-do you th-th-think so Aegie? R-r-really?"

"Do you trust me Onny?"

"O-o-oh yes Aegie! I w-w-will always tr-tr-trust you!"

Onny reached out to his brother, and in that precious moment, the two brothers hugged each other tenderly.

"Come on Onny, what do say we go for a ride on my horse and get some air in the lungs? What do you say little brother?"

Oh, yes Ae-Ae-Aegie. I l-l-love riding with you. After all y-you are Ar-Ar-Archi-p-p-as! The m-m-master of horses ... and now a f-f-free man! Let's go b-b-big brother!"

∽

Chapter Fourteen

A Dying

Wish

~

Circa AD 56

*N*ews continue to spread around the province about a new faith movement sweeping through Asia Minor. The Greeks had their gods. The Romans had their gods. The Jews had their faith in one God they called Yahweh — the God of Abraham, Issac and Jacob. But although this new faith had its origins in the Jewish religion, it was quite different to them all.

The people of this new movement were quickly becoming known as Christians — followers of the one they called Jesus the Christ. One of the major leaders of this movement was a man named Paul, who had been travelling throughout Asia Minor spreading the message of this new faith. He had earned a controversial reputation for persuading many people to join this movement, while at the same time stirring up dissent among many of the Jewish leaders.

There appeared to be much interest among many of the Greek women, which is why Nikolette's cousin Claudia, urged her before she passed away, to seek out this man called Paul, and listen to what he had to say about Jesus.

Recently, it had come to Nikolette's attention that this Apostle Paul was once again visiting the region. She had spoken with her son about her interest in meeting Paul, and her desire to hear firsthand, and what there was about his message that was changing individual lives and communities.

At the time, Philemon seemed quite indifferent to his mother's suggestion. He was not at all interested in hearing any news of this new faith — after all, the gods had been good to him, and there was no need for another god. He was prosperous and well-respected in the Laodicean business community.

Nikolette was determined to convince her son to at least extend an invitation to the itinerant preacher Paul. "My son, I do not ask much of you, even as I am getting older. But I have a strong sense in my heart that this man has something very important to share with us. Why not send Archippas with some horses to find Paul and offer him your personal invitation to visit us?

"Mitéra, I will consider your request," replied Philemon.

"Philemon, my son, do not delay too long. I have a strong sense that this Paul — will bring life-changing blessings to us … to you and to this oikos. If you procrastinate, you may miss out altogether. At least hear him speak — hear him out — and if you don't like what he has to say, about this new faith … then you can ask him to leave."

That night, Phil could hardly sleep. He was disturbed in his mind and his spirit. The next morning, he was about to inform his mother of his decision to send for Paul. As he made his way to his mother's bedchamber, her personal servant raced toward him, weeping and wailing. "Kyrios! Kyrios! Your mitéra is dead! She must have died in her sleep during the night."

He ran to her room and flung himself down beside her bed. Falling to his knees, he wept bitterly, grief-stricken not only by her sudden passing but also by the realization that he, too, was now an orphan — just like Apphie and Archie.

The oikos was immediately thrown into chaos as Phil and Apphie tried to console each other, while also directing their staff in preparation for Nikolette's funeral. Everything was put on hold, and all focus turned to arranging the prothesis and laying out the body for viewing.

Much like their wedding celebrations, this funeral and its rituals were unconventional in many ways. Apphia and Philemon led the mourning together, including the ritual wailing and the funeral procession. Every detail was adapted, yet handled with deep respect.

Their month of mourning proceeded as would be expected with the set visitations to the graveside. During this time of mourning Phil and Apphie supported each other as best they could, but Phil was troubled by his mother's last comments regarding the preacher man, Paul. Her words haunted him day and night: "*Philemon, my son, do not delay too long. I have a strong sense that this Paul — will bring life-changing blessings to you and this oikos. But if you procrastinate, you may miss out altogether.*"

On the final evening of the official mourning period, Phil shared with Archie about his mother's last words and his deep regret at not acting sooner. He spoke with great respect about his love for her and how much he had appreciated her guidance throughout his life. Now, it was time to fulfill her dying wish.

Philemon handed Archie a handwritten, sealed invitation to deliver to the preacher Paul. He also instructed him to carry his certificate of freedom and his certificate of name change as a precaution against being apprehended by Roman soldiers. It was agreed that Archie was to depart at daybreak the next morning.

✍

Contemplations for Individual Reflection and Group Discussion

CHAPTER #13:

- Think about the time you have been given an opportunity, but you knew that it would impact your family. How did you handle the situation?
- Think about when someone you know has been given a promotion or an award, and you missed out. What was your response?

CHAPTER #14:

- Have you ever had someone make a dying wish that involved you?
- Have you ever had a conversation with someone only to realise that you were the last person they spoke with before they unexpectedly died?

CHAPTER FIFTEEN

ON A

MISSION

*T*he next morning, Archippas rode out on horseback, leading two other horses. Rumour had it that Paul was making his way through the region, but exactly where? That was the *master of horses's* first challenge. At every stop along the way, he would casually inquire about the whereabouts of the preacher.

Eventually, he came across a small party of travellers heading toward Colossae. They knew of Paul and mentioned that they'd passed him and his companions on the road from Antioch. He thanked them for the information and headed off in the direction they had indicated.

Even with two extra horses, Archie moved quickly, and after some time, he came across a group that he hoped would be Paul and his friends, Silas and Timothy. It was already past midday, but by Archie's estimate, they still had enough time to reach Laodicea before sunset if they moved swiftly.

Archie approached the trio of travellers slowly, drew the horses to a holt, dismounted and proceeded to make conversation. "Greetings to you," he said with a broad smile showing his very white teeth.

"Greetings friend," replied Paul. "Are you looking for someone or just passing through?"

"Sir, I am trying to find a preacher called Paul — the one called the Apostle," enquired Archie.

"Look no further friend, for I am he!" replied Paul. "What is it that you require of me ... um?" Paul gestured as if to imply that the master of horses should introduce himself.

"Forgive me sir, my birth name is Aegeus. I was born a slave in the oikos of Dolion and his son Philemon. A few years ago my master changed my name to Archippas. And more recently, I was granted my freedom and now work as Philemon's personal assistant. Here ..." He took out his certificates from under his cloak and handed them to Paul. "Here are my certifications with Philemon's own seal."

Paul examined them carefully just like he was a legal person. Then he rolled them up and handed them back to Archie. "Archippas, it is a pleasure to meet you. Let me introduce my companions, Silas and Timothy." They all nodded in formal recognition of each other.

"So what should we call you young man? Archippas — 'Master of Horses', Aegeus or just Freedman?" Turning to his friends he added, "And I thought I had enough titles!" Silas and Timothy laughed jovially, as did Archie — even though it was more out of politeness, since he was not sure if they were laughing about him or about Paul's comment.

"Sir, if you will ... you can call me Archie, as I am quite used to being called that by my master — oh, I mean by Philemon. We have been friends since my birth. Although my younger brother still calls me Aegie!"

"Right! Archie it is!" said Paul. "And you Archie, can simply call me Paul — though I also had a name change. I used to be called Saul ... but that's a story for another time!" Paul declared. Then he added, "Now that we have all the formalities out of the way, tell us — what is so important that you've ridden all this way ... and with two extra horses. Hey?

"But before you explain why you've interrupted our journey, please, let's sit. Come, drink, and break bread, shall we?" Paul added.

"But sir — I mean, Paul — I don't mean any disrespect ..." Archie protested. "... but if we were to leave now, we could be in Laodicea before sunset!"

"Oh! I see!" Paul said, motioning to the others to sit on the grass beside the road. "Tell me, Archie ... what's the hurry? And did you say ... Laodicea?"

Archie sat down albeit reluctantly, as he could tell that neither Paul, nor the others were in any hurry to get moving. He began his explanation of why he been commissioned to seek Paul and extend Philemon's invitation to visit.

"As far as I understand the situation Paul, Philemon's mother recently passed away quite suddenly. And the night before she died, she pleaded with her son to seek you out and invite you to come and speak. Apparently she had heard many stories of changed lives with a new faith experience. Her friends in Colossae had been talking about a group of Christians meeting under the leadership of someone called Epaphras — I think that's how you pronounce it?"

"Epaphras, you say!?" Paul acknowledged. "Yes, he's a good man. Very solid in his faith and teaching about Jesus Christ. We've met a few times and had a number of discussions ... and seen many answers to prayer." Paul paused for a moment and then changed the subject. "By the way Archie, I'm very impressed how well you speak perfect Greek ... for an African slave ... sorry ... a freed African slave, that is!"

"Thank you sir. I also had a very good teacher in Philemon, from the time I began to talk," replied Archie.

"So then," asked Paul, "what may I ask was Philemon's mother's final request?"

"Well ..." Archie paused, "I was getting to that Paul. The night before she died ... and just to make it clear ... she was not ill at all. Just pleading with her son as Kyrios, to extend the invitation to you. She made him promise that he would do everything he could to track you down and ask you to come to their oikos.

"She told Philemon that he needed to hear what you had to say about this new faith, that was spreading quickly throughout Asia." Archie took a breath as he anticipated Paul's response.

However, it was Timothy who spoke up. "So Archie, what did Philemon actually say ... not knowing that this would be his mother's dying wish?"

Archie continued. "At first he was not interested. In fact, he told me later that he'd tried to change the subject at least three times, but she was a very determined woman. He promised that he would think about it overnight."

"When did she die?" enquired Silas.

"That very night was four weeks ago, but everything was put on hold for our thirty days of mourning."

Silas prodded further, "So ... was Philemon intending to send for Paul or not, or is he now just trying to appease what turned out to be his mother's death wish?"

"Great question, Silas," Archie explained, "As I understand it, apparently he did not sleep well that night. Something stirred in his mind, and so even before he found out that his mother had died during the night, he had already decided that he would follow his mother's desire to invite Paul to come.

"Last night, was the final day of the mourning period, and his wife reminded him of his mother's request." Archie paused as he looked directly at Paul, "She said that she had heard rumours that you and your friends were on your way to Macedonia."

Paul smiled as he said, "Wow! News travels faster than us these days!" Everyone laughed. "However, unfortunately, we were not planning on going via Laodicea, nevertheless we will see what the Lord says about that overnight."

"But sirs," protested Archie. "I've brought horses ... so if we leave now, we could still be back before sunset."

"Now Archie," Paul calmly said. "If we are meant to go with you, then it will be revealed in the Lord's time ... in His way ... and for His purpose. We will know in the morning!"

Archie looked at Paul and then the others ... perplexed.

෨

Chapter Sixteen

Campfire

Stories

$\mathcal{S}$ilas and Timothy stood up and began gathering some wood to start a fire. "I guess we are camping here for the night" he said rhetorically. Archie you can get the fire going."

Without overthinking it, Archie also stood to gather some kindling and, using his flintstone, had a small fire going by the time the others returned with thicker pieces of dried wood. As he tended the fire, he became suddenly aware of how calm and friendly these three men were — completely unphased and unhurried. At the same time, he also felt Paul's gaze on him, yet he remained at ease. He reconciled himself to the reality that these men, were sincere in their faith and truly men of peace.

Timothy organized their sleeping mats while Silas cooked dough and dried meat mixed with herbs and olives. As they ate and talked, time seemed to drift away. Afternoon turned to evening, and the conversation around the crackling campfire became increasingly dominated by Paul.

He was, in every sense, a wordsmith — crafting questions, telling stories, and sharing his message of faith about the one he called Jesus Christ. Though difficult to grasp at first, as he continued to speak, his words began to make sense ... even to young Archie.

Paul explained, "You see Archie, I too was once a slave."

"You were?!" Archie's face lit up like a spark from the campfire. "You're kidding me right?!"

Paul smiled warmly. "No, I am not kidding, Archie. I was once a man who persecuted the followers of Jesus. I was a Pharisee in the Jewish faith — an expert in the Law. I was bound by the Law, zealously determined to make a name for myself."

"Then I started hearing stories about Jesus of Nazareth — a miracle healer and preacher who was crucified by the Romans and reportedly rose from the dead. The more I heard about this man and his followers, the more I hated them. In turn, I became even more determined to eradicate them before their movement grew out of control," Paul continued.

Archie interjected, "But what — or who — were you a slave too, Paul? You did say that you were a slave, did you not?"

"Oh yes, Archie," Paul replied. "I was a slave to the Jewish Law — it had to be obeyed — and these followers of Jesus were breaking laws left, right, and centre! The Law had been established for centuries! You could also say I was a slave to control, so much so that I sought permission from my overseers to pursue, persecute, and imprison — even exterminate — these new believers who were turning the world upside down."

Archie's eyes widened with amazement. He was hooked. He needed to know more. Even in the fading light the others could see the whites of his eyes. "But how could someone like you have been a slave and then become such a wise and free man?!" he exclaimed.

Archie listened intently as Paul shared the story of his life's transformation. Paul chuckled softly as he began, "The journey of life is full of unexpected turns, my young friend. When someone is enslaved to sin, they obey sin, which becomes their master. This type of slavery starts with just one sin. And in my case, Archie, it was self-righteousness.

"I learned the hard way that we are not sinners because we break the Law — we break the Law because we are sinners.

"As a zealous Jew of the Pharisee sect, I once believed it was my duty to actively oppose the name of Jesus of Nazareth. In fact, as the number of his believers — who were originally called 'The Way'—increased, I carried out this opposition in Jerusalem by imprisoning many devout followers under the authority of the chief priests. Furthermore, I cast my vote against them, leading to their death sentences.

"In my zeal, I frequently punished them in Jewish synagogues, trying to compel them to blaspheme. My self-righteous anger boiled over as I relentlessly pursued them, even travelling to distant cities to continue their persecution.

"It was during one such mission to Damascus, authorized by the chief priests, that something extraordinary happened. While traveling along the road at midday, a light brighter than the sun suddenly flashed from heaven, surrounding me and those who accompanied me.

"The light was so intense that I was blinded for some time. We all fell to the ground, and I heard a voice speaking to me in Aramaic: '*Saul, Saul, why are you persecuting me? Your resistance is only causing you harm.*'

"I asked, 'Who-o-o are you, Lord?'

"The voice replied, '*I am Jesus, the one you are persecuting. Now stand up and go into the city, to a certain man's house, where you will receive your sight back and further instructions. For I have appeared to you in order to reveal your purpose and commission to you as my servant. You will bear witness to what you have seen and to the truths I will reveal to you in the future.*'

"Before I was led into Damascus as a blind man, the voice concluded, '*I will protect you from the persecution of your own people and from the hostility of other nations to whom I will send you. Your mission will be to open their eyes to their true condition, leading them from darkness to light and from the power of Satan to God. Through faith in me, they will receive forgiveness of sins and be set free, inheriting the blessings I have promised my children.*'"

Archie sat in silence, absorbing the profound words as the fire flickered, casting dancing shadows on the faces of the men who had become his unexpected companions. Then Paul concluded, "Archie, it is only through faith in Jesus and His grace, that we find our true path. Perhaps, one day — even tonight — you too will experience such a transformation!"

Archie felt numb with intrigue and excitement, and he fumbled for words. "I would never want to hurt anyone — except for Kyrios Dolion, for the pain he caused my family — especially my Emaye and Abaye. My parents both died when I was about twelve years old because of what he did to my mother. I'm not sure your Jesus could forgive him for what he did — or forgive me for my anger toward him!

Without any hesitation Paul declared "Oh but Archie, He can! Even when Jesus was being crucified He prayed: 'Father, forgive them, for they do not understand what they are doing!' He was referring not only to the Roman soldiers, who nailed Him to the cross, but also to the Chief Priests, Pharisees and others arranged for His mock trial before Pontius Pilate and Herod. If Jesus can forgive them Archie, then my young friend, there is no doubt He can forgive you ... and even your former master!"

"Maybe ..." Archie replied, raising his voice slightly so that it resonated in the cool evening air. "But I do not think I could forgive him — he doesn't deserve it!"

Paul waited a moment, allowing the echo of Archie's voice to fade into the night. "I understand. And I did not deserve forgiveness either. I was the chief of sinners — yet Jesus showed me mercy and forgiveness.

"Despite the fact that I was once a blasphemer — slandering the things of God — a persecutor, and a violent aggressor."

Archie looked away in order to take in what he'd just heard. Then Paul added, "Archie you're absolutely right — you cannot forgive your former master … in your own strength. Only Jesus can help you do that.

"All you have to do is confess with your mouth that Jesus Christ is Lord, and believe in your heart that He died for your sins and rose from the dead to give you new life and hope. Confess your sins before Him, receive His forgiveness, and be filled with the Holy Spirit. Only Jesus can do it Archie!

"Oh, one more thing Archie. Forgiveness is not about letting your former Kyrios off the hook. But rather it is about providing you the opportunity to move forward. By forgiving, you can let go of the anger and the hurt."

There was an extended silence filled with awkward anticipation as the darkness of the night enveloped the small group. Archie finally broke the silence, as if he had not heard anything Paul had just said.

"So, Paul ... are you coming to speak with Philemon tomorrow?" he asked matter-of-factly.

Paul replied politely, "We'll sleep on it, and see what the Lord says in the morning. Good night, my friends." With that, Paul lay down and rolled over.

"Good night," each one replied in turn.

Archie lay back on his bed mat, staring at the stars. He remained there for quite some time, contemplating what he had just heard. Sleep eluded him — he tossed and turned, unable to shake Paul's challenging, life-changing story from his mind.

∽

Contemplations for Individual Reflection and Group Discussion

CHAPTER #15:

- Think about a time when you have set out to meet someone whom you have never met or didn't even knew what they looked like. What was that like? Did you actually meet up with them?

CHAPTER #16:

- Campfire conversations can provide insights into people's personalities. Why is that? Have you ever gathered around a campfire, sharing stories in an atmosphere of openness?
- Recall the first time you heard somebody share their testimony of faith in Jesus.
- When was the first time you were challenged with forgiving someone who'd had a major impact on your life? How did you go about that?
- Can you think of a time when the best decision was 'to sleep on it'?

CHAPTER SEVENTEEN

A CHANGE

OF HEART

*P*aul was up at the crack of dawn. The birds were singing, and the scent of fresh flatbread filled the air.

Timothy, Silas, and Archie woke up, taking in their surroundings in the morning light. The fire's warmth enveloped them and the aroma of bread filled their nostrils.

"So, Paul, what's it gonna be?" Archie asked abruptly. "Are you coming to Laodicea or not?"

"Well, good morning to you too, Archie!" Paul replied with a chuckle. He let the question hang for a moment, then sighed. "Actually, I thought you might have said something else first, seeing as you had a pretty restless night! Even talking in your sleep, as it turns out!"

Archie's face flushed — even though no-one could see due to his dark skin. "Good morning Paul. Sorry!" he said sheepishly. "Yeah, I didn't get much sleep at all because I couldn't stop thinking about your story. I didn't doze off until after I'd had a long conversation with Jesus."

"Really? Tell us more!" Timothy urged, leaning forward.

Archie hesitated for a moment, then nodded. "Yeah ... well ... I realized I needed Jesus to forgive me and help me become a better person."

"That's awesome, Archie!" the others chorused together.

Paul stood and reached out to help Archie up. As Archie grasped his hand, Paul pulled him into a firm embrace. "Welcome to the family, my new brother in the faith!" he said warmly. "Come on you guys … join in!"

Timothy and Silas grinned at each other before stepping forward to join them. One by one, they embraced Archie, welcoming him into their brotherhood.

"Now, to answer your question, Archie," Paul began, "I didn't get much sleep either. The Lord was warning me in a dream not to go any further into Asia at this time. I've discerned that the timing is not right for me to enter Bithynia, which means we'll need to adjust our plans. So, that does give us enough time to divert to Laodicea — at least for a couple of days."

With a broad smile, his white teeth contrasting against his dark skin, Archie nodded in approval. "I take that as a yes!" Then he said, "I'm hungry! Thanks for the bread, Paul!"

∾

Once they had finished eating breakfast and packed up camp, the four men mounted the horses and headed along the dusty road towards Laodicea.

As there were only three horses, Timothy — being the youngest and the lightest of Archie's new friends — rode tandem with Archie, who led the small pack of horses at a steady pace with the intention of arriving before midday.

Upon arriving at the oikos estate, Philemon and Apphia were eating and drinking on their portico. The horsemen dismounted and were greeted by their hosts. Although Philemon was still somewhat indifferent to the purpose of their 'good-news' visit, he was very hospitable. Inwardly, he consoled himself with the fact that he was simply paying respect to his mother's final wishes.

Philemon ordered his servants to fetch water and towels for the men to freshen up after their journey. Once the visitors' feet had been washed and their faces refreshed, and the normal formalities of greeting were over, they were offered seats, bread, and wine — which they gladly accepted.

Apphia couldn't help but notice Archie's demeanour. There was something quite different about him — as if there were a radiance about his face. She was just about to ask him a question when, suddenly, Phil collapsed to the floor and began convulsing erratically. His face swelled, and his head jerked and thrashed from side to side.

CHAPTER EIGHTEEN

IT'S A

MIRACLE

*A*pphie screamed, her voice piercing the tranquil air as she rushed to her husband's side. Her heart pounded furiously in her chest, and her hands trembled as she tried to steady his thrashing form. The serene atmosphere of the estate was shattered by her anguished cries, echoing through the portico and reverberating in the hearts of all present.

Servants raced to the scene from every direction to see what the chaos was about. Archie came alongside to support Apphia in her panicked state. The servants stood around helplessly, watching; while Paul, Silas, and Timothy stood back, observing.

Philemon's face continued to swell until, after several moments, the convulsions suddenly ceased. A deathly silence hovered over the scene. The Kyrios appeared dead. Nobody moved. Everyone was in deep shock.

Without saying a word, Paul moved slowly towards Philemon's motionless body. He knelt down beside his host, and gently placed his hands on Philemon's chest. There appeared to be a silent understanding between the visitors as Silas and Timothy also knelt down beside Paul.

Paul was praying ever so quietly. Silas and Timothy seamlessly placed their hands on Paul's shoulders ... and then to everyone's astonishment, Archie joined them as he too knelt down and placed his hand on Timothy's shoulder.

Every one of the onlookers collectively held their breath in anticipation — not just of what was happening, but more importantly, of what was expected to happen. No one moved. There was a pregnant silence as this group of men prayed quietly — for a couple of minutes, or maybe five.

Occasionally, Apphia could distinguish some of the words being whispered in prayer. Some of the words she could hear repeated were: "*In Jesus' name! In Jesus' name!*"

Then, without warning, Philemon's body suddenly jolted several inches off the floor — as if he'd been struck by lightning. He gasped for breath and sat bolt upright. When at last he could focus, he found himself looking directly into the smiling, bearded face of the Apostle Paul.

Everyone gasped in astonishment. "It's a miracle! He's alive!" The servants were ecstatically declaring, "It's a miracle! This visitor must be a god!". They were all jumping around with such excitement and joy.

Paul assisted Philemon to his feet, and to everyone's surprise, the Kyrios embraced the Apostle as if he were a long-lost friend.

The cacophony of rejoicing escalated until Archie stood up motioned for them to stop and listen to what he had to say. "These men are my friends; this man Paul is not a god as you think. He represents the one true God whose name is Jesus. The miracle you saw here is because he — *we* — prayed in the name of Jesus Christ."

Everyone was amazed at Archie's declaration of faith, which brought a calm reassurance and expectancy to every one present. As the servants bustled about to clean up the disarray of tables and spillage, one of the servants discovered a bee in the Kyrios' wine chalice. It was also noted that the bee was missing it's stinger, and so it was concluded then that the bee must have stung Philemon on the tongue which caused an instantaneous allergic reaction.

Once the situation had resumed to some sense of order, more food was ordered for the celebrations to continue.

❦

Contemplations for Individual Reflection and Group Discussion

CHAPTERS #17 & #18:

- Has there ever been a moment when you observed something different about another person — either good or bad? Or perhaps they observed something different about you?
- What do you think of prayer being a first-aid response … rather than a last resort?
- Have you ever witnessed a miracle? How did you respond?

... I AM ONESIMUS

CHAPTER NINETEEN

FAREWELL

BLESSINGS

*D*uring the course of the afternoon, Philemon, Apphia, and Archie listened intently as Paul, Silas, and Timothy each shared their personal stories of how they became followers of Jesus. Every story left a deep impact, and even though Archie had already heard Paul's testimony before, it still resonated deeply within him.

After what felt like hours of discussion, with the visitors answering question after question, the time came for Paul to turn his attention to Philemon. Getting straight to the point, he asked, "Tell me, friend, would I be correct in saying that you weren't keen on inviting me here at all, were you, Philemon?"

Philemon shifted uncomfortably, appearing somewhat embarrassed. "To be honest, Paul, I had no interest whatsoever in hearing what you had to say about Jesus of Nazareth ..."

Paul interjected quickly. "But you felt guilty because, as it turned out, it was your mother's dying wish. Hmm?"

"You're absolutely correct on both counts Paul," Philemon admitted. "But now ... I must say ... I owe you! You saved my life! Thank you."

Paul continued, "You could say that my new friend, but more correctly... you owe Jesus. After today's death-defying event, you can no longer bury your head in the sand and ignore the fact that it was Jesus who brought you back to life through the power of the Holy Spirit. You are physically alive only because His power was working through us.

"Jesus has gotten your attention today, Philemon, but what about your soul, hey? He wants more — He wants you. He could easily have taken your life, but He chose to give it back to you, because He desires for you to truly live. He wants all of you — to be fully alive!

"Let me put it this way: Philemon, do you believe that Jesus Christ is the Son of the living God, who has the power to save you — not just from physical death, but from eternal death? Will you confess with your mouth and believe in your heart that you are a sinner in need of His saving grace? Will you accept Him today, as your Lord and Saviour?"

Philemon looked at his wife, then at Archie. The smile beaming from Archie's face radiated such joy and peace — something Philemon had never seen before. Apphia searched Philemon's expression and body language. She was bursting at the seams, eager to express her own desire to put her faith in Jesus, but she held back, allowing her husband to take the lead. As he looked at her, he could see it in her eyes.

Philemon moved out of his seat and knelt beside Paul. "What must I do, Paul?" Tears streamed down his face. "What does Jesus really want from me?"

At that moment, Apphie also came and knelt beside her husband in support and agreement.

Placing his hands on Philemon's chest, as he had done earlier in the day, Paul said, "My friend, earlier today, Jesus gave you your life back — now He wants you to give your life over to Him. Your whole life — body, mind, and spirit — everything you have. Just tell Him. Surrender it all to Him, and He will fill you with His Spirit."

Philemon drew his wife closer. Hand in hand, they submitted their lives to Jesus, asking for the Holy Spirit to fill them. Immediately, the Spirit fell upon the small group gathered under the portico. A deep, awe-inspiring awareness of God's presence filled the space, stretching the moment into what felt like hours. There was much praising, repenting, and praying — both in their native language and in unknown tongues.

᪗

Paul and his friends were welcomed as guests into the oikos for the next two days, as Philemon, Apphia, and Archie sat like sponges, soaking up every drop of living water that Paul taught them — ably supported by Silas and Timothy.

When it came time for them to leave, Philemon showered them with ample supplies for the next leg of their missionary journey.

Saying goodbye wasn't easy, as such a strong bond had been forged between Paul and his companions and Philemon's family in such a short time.

It had become customary for Paul to pronounce blessings over people as part of any farewell — whether they were individuals or church gatherings. With Timothy still in training, he was keen to observe what was about to take place.

Standing up, Paul was filled with the Spirit and prophesied over Philemon and Apphia. He pronounced God's blessing of peace, favour and commission, following on from what had transpired over the last two days, to establish and care for a house church gathering.

"Your mother's dying wish was that this family might experience the life-changing grace of the Lord Jesus Christ. What has occurred here in such a short amount of time has not been by accident, but providentially by God's hand in His perfect timing.

"Philemon and Apphia, the Lord knows your hearts. You have both been called to be faithful witnesses to what He has done and what He will continue to do in good times and bad."

At this point, Silas spoke directly to Archie. "The Holy Spirit wants you to know, Archippas, that just as Jesus declared to Simon the fisherman, 'You are Peter, the rock,' so too Aegeus ... 'protector, and now master of horses' ... you will have a double role of being protector of your brothers — who are still slaves and servants. Teach them to respect their masters by putting Jesus first, as if they were serving Jesus Himself.

"As master of horses, your task is also to minister to masters — especially those who are ruthless and unbridled in the way they treat their slaves and servants."

With their prophetic blessings having been pronounced, Paul, Silas, and Timothy departed.

❧

CHAPTER TWENTY

SPREADING OF

NEWFOUND

FAITH

Circa AD 58-59

In the days that followed, Philemon and Apphia eagerly shared their newfound faith in Jesus throughout the Laodicean community. Before long, they were hosting regular gatherings for new believers at the oikos.

These meetings had no set format, but they centred on sharing testimonies and discussing who Jesus was — His teachings and miracles, His death and resurrection, His ascension, and His promised return. They also explored the baptism of the Holy Spirit, speaking in tongues, repentance, and baptisms by immersion. At every gathering, they shared food and fellowship and also celebrated the Lord's Supper.

The people lifted their praises to God — the King of Kings, the Creator — for His saving grace and the risen Lord. They had much to be thankful for, yet so much to learn. With each new understanding learned, came the need to unlearn and release old pagan Greek superstitions and practices.

❧

Meanwhile, Archie eagerly shared the story of his conversion with fellow slaves and servants. As he did, he encouraged them to respect their masters, reminding them that in doing so, they were honouring God. His ministry had its challenges, as many slaves and servants were deeply bound in both heart and mind, and some took offence at the fact that he was now a freed man (*libertinus*).

They struggled to reconcile how a loving and forgiving God could set them free in their hearts while they remained slaves to their masters. Nor could they grasp the truth that Paul had shared with Archie: that in Christ, there is neither slave nor free, Jew or Gentile … we are all one.

Archie tried unsuccessfully, to explain how Paul often used the analogy of slaves to show how believers should conform to Jesus' will. He also recalled Paul saying, "A life of sin is slavery, while obedience to God is true service and freedom."

Most notably, he remembered Paul saying that anyone is a 'slave' to whatever they choose to obey or let control them. Paul often reminded his listeners that freedom meant 'being free *from* something in order to be free *for* something.'

Archie also recalled Paul mentioning Epaphras in Colossae. Epaphras, the founder of the Colossian church, was recognized by Paul as a *faithful minister of Christ*. Mentored by Paul, he played a crucial role in spreading the Gospel as a *fellow servant* and *servant of Christ Jesus*. So, with Phil's permission, Archie was able to travel to Colossae and meet with Epaphras.

As a result of the connection with Epaphras and Archie's positive report to Phil, Epaphras was invited to Laodicea to teach the small gathering of new Christians regularly. A strong, supportive relationship was soon established between the Colossian church and the Laodicean house church.

Although the gospel spread quickly and was well received among Laodicean Greeks, many new believers struggled to abandon their Greek superstitions and pagan practices. Over time, this led to a fusion of pagan rituals with Christian traditions, including prayer, baptism, and the Lord's Supper.

In addition, many wealthy Laodicean believers were reluctant to relinquish the hold of prosperity — money and property — over their lives. Though generous givers overall, they still let the god of mammon hold sway in their daily lives, contradicting their newfound faith in the one true God — the faithful provider of all things good.

∽

Since his conversion, Archie had tried several times to share his newfound faith with Onny, but his brother remained disinterested. This was partly because they were spending less time together, and also because Aegie — now Archie — was a *libertinus*. Onny's heart however had grown hardened and bitter, not only toward the Kyrios Phil, but also towards his wendme (brother).

With his simple, stammering words, Onny could only express that, although he was happy for his wendme, he believed there was no hope for change for himself at all. It felt like a hopeless situation for such a useless slave.

For so many years now, he'd heard Kyrios tell him, both directly and indirectly, that he was useless — even though, at first, he didn't like it or accept it. However, over time, it started to wear him down, and eventually, he came to believe that he was just that — useless, with no hope of change. With this mindset, his stuttering worsened, as did his self-conscious awareness of his clumsiness.

Archie was deeply grieved by his brother's resistance to the gospel message, as he had always loved and tried to protect his younger wendme. But now, he felt as though he had let Onny down in many ways. The close bond and open communication they'd always shared and enjoyed were no longer evident, and he despaired at his inability to connect with Onny on his level of understanding. All he could do was pray, asking the Lord to soften his brother's heart and grant him wisdom to know what to do.

Sensing the Lord's prompting, he sought a private moment to confide in Apphia, knowing that the subject of Onny had always been a touchy one with Philemon. He shared his concerns about Onny's downcast and bitter spirit, as well as his unwillingness to hear about new life in Jesus.

The Lord had already prepared the way by softening Apphia's heart to listen. She assured him that the Lord had given her a plan. She also mentioned she had heard that Paul was under house arrest in Rome.

Apphia also encouraged Archie, affirming his obedience and concern for Onny. The Lord had shown her that Onny needed to meet Paul and spend some time with him. With Archie approaching her, it was the confirmation she needed — she was convinced this was God's plan for Onny.

She cautioned that, for security reasons, she was not at liberty to discuss any further details of the plan. They agreed that neither of them would say anything to Philemon or Onny.

Before parting, she added, "Archie, I sincerely believe the Lord's will shall be done ... in His way ... in His time."

"Amen?" Archie said with conviction.

He thanked Apphia for her willingness to listen — to him and to the Spirit. Then he left the oikos and returned to his responsibilities — checking on the horses and managing other administrative tasks.

Archie felt relieved that the Lord had gone before him, and that Apphia was in tune with the Holy Spirit. Archie's heart and mind were settled knowing that the Lord was already working in ways that he could not see or understand.

Contemplations for Individual Reflection and Group Discussion

CHAPTER #19:

- Think about a time when you've heard "I owe you." What does that mean, really? Consider this excerpt from a song:

  'He paid a debt he did not owe;

  I owed a debt I could not pay
  I needed someone to wash my sins away
  And now I sing a brand new song,

  "Amazing grace" … the whole day long,
  Christ Jesus paid the debt that I could never pay'

- Has there ever been a time when you realised that God has got your attention?
- What is it like to sit and soak in new teaching?
- Have you ever received a prophetic word spoken over you?

CHAPTER #20:

- What was it like sharing your faith with someone close to you for the first time? How was it received?
- Have you experienced or witnessed other struggle in leaving past habits or beliefs behind?

... I AM ONESIMUS

CHAPTER TWENTY-ONE

THE CASE OF THE

MISSING SLAVE

$\mathcal{T}$he next day, Archie wanted to touch base with Onny again. Expecting to find him in the fields, he was surprised when Onny was nowhere to be seen. Some of the other slaves informed him that Onny was gone.

"What do you mean, gone? Gone where?" he demanded.

"We don't know, Aegie — Archie!" one of them replied. "All we know is that when it was time to get out of bed this morning, he was gone ... that's all we know! We don't know where or why. Oh, and he was late coming to bed last night."

Archie was perplexed and deeply worried for his brother's safety. Given Onny's clumsiness and speech impediment, it was out of character for him to venture too far from familiar surroundings — especially unaccompanied.

Without hesitation, Archie reported Onny's disappearance to Philemon. Though Phil secretly felt relieved at the thought of no longer having to endure Onny's presence and embarrassment; he instructed Archie to first organize a search party to go around the estate. If Onny was not found, they would then expand the search into the city.

Archie scoured the entire property on horseback, accompanied by a few of the slaves, but to no avail. He then expanded his search, combing the areas between the estate and the city. He searched everywhere — up and down every street, through every market stall, temple and synagogue.

After three days of searching, Archie was beside himself. Upon returning to the oikos in distress, he sought out Apphia, knowing she had listened to him just days before. He believed she would hear him again — and perhaps have a word from the Lord.

"Apphia, where could Onny have gone by himself?" he questioned, his voice breaking as tears welled in his eyes. "He's never done anything like this before. This is just so uncharacteristic of him!"

The moment was awkward for Apphia. She couldn't afford to take on Archie's emotional burden, yet she tried to console him. She reminded him that the Lord's ways were higher than man's ways, and so He surely had a purpose in all this. She could not risk taking him into her confidence any further at this time. "All will be revealed in the Lord's time. Trust Him, Archie. Let's believe that your brother is in good hands. We will be praying for you and Onny!"

❦

After gathering his thoughts and emotions together, Archie thanked Apphia for her wisdom and kindness, then he went back to his routine duties. It was, however, difficult for him to focus on what he should be doing with the burden of his brother's welfare at stake.

After Archie had left the portico, Apphia sat and reflected on her discreet scheme, which she had implemented with much precision since their last conversation.

The Lord had instructed her to write a letter to Paul, explaining their concerns about Onny's well-being — including his resistance to the gospel. In the letter, she detailed Onny's story, revealing that he was Philemon's half-brother, a fact Phil refused to acknowledge or discuss. She explained that most of what she knew about Onny's past had come from discussions with Phil's mother, as well as from conversations with Archie and her own observations.

She acknowledged that Philemon was, in general, a kind and loving man — true to the meaning of his name. But his distaste for Onny ... his deep-seated resentment and rejection of him were starting to affect their ministry. Despite leading the church gatherings in their oikos, this unresolved bitterness toward his brother's mixed-heritage needed to be addressed.

Apphia described the cruel words of humiliation, criticism, and rejection that Philemon frequently used when speaking of Onny — words that had wounded him for years. This pattern had begun even long before Philemon discovered they shared the same father, stretching back to Onny's toddler years.

Since Paul had never met Onny during his visit to Laodicea, Apphia was unable to warn him of the unmistakable resemblance between Onny and Philemon. She chuckled at the thought of Paul's surprised reaction when they would eventually meet.

She also wrote of Archie's deep distress, explaining that he was beside himself with worry and praying fervently for his brother. She requested that Paul not mention anything about her letter if he intended to write to Philemon. She especially stressed that he should not say anything initially to Onny, but wait for the Lord's leading — empathizing with the fact that Onny needed to find his true identity. By spending time with Paul, she hoped, Onny might also come to know Christ as his Saviour and Lord.

Unbeknownst to Philemon, she was fully aware that he had been deliberately short-changing Onny's wages for many years. Therefore, as part of her discreet plan, she went to the money safe and took out a considerable amount of money — essentially enough to cover any costs of food or lodging that Onny might incur on his journey to Rome.

In addition to the letter and the cash, Apphia also wrote out a certificate of leave and permission to travel, sealing it with

Philemon's own waxen seal, just in case Onny was detained or accused of being a run-away slave.

Apphia was fully aware of Onny's lack of literacy skills, unlike Archie, who had been tutored by Philemon since he could speak. Therefore, she had no hesitation in entrusting these documents to Onny to carry to Rome.

Her plan unfolded without a hitch. At midnight, the night before Onny was reported missing, Apphia had given instructions to her personal assistant to awaken Onny without being detected by anyone and escort him as far as Ephesus. Once there, he was to seek out one of the family's contacts, who would then escort Onny the rest of the way to Rome to find Paul in house arrest. Her assistant was to report back to her immediately upon his return to confirm that the first part of the plan had been carried out successfully.

Just before midnight, Onny was gently woken by Apphia's assistant, with the filtered moonlight shining through a gap in the roof. He motioned for Onny to remain quiet and follow him. Being a compliant but also somewhat naïve slave, Onny did not hesitate to accompany Apphia's assistant. Once outside and away from the sleeping quarters, the assistant quickly explained, "Onny, the Kyrios' wife — my Despoina (mistress) — is sending us on a secret mission to Rome to deliver a package to a man in prison. Onny, she has chosen you because of your trustworthy character. Come on, we must leave immediately!"

Despite being woken from his sleep, Onny was alert enough to take in what he was hearing, and for the first time in his life he felt a pang of usefulness. The air was crisp and still. The two men quietly led their horses to the edge of the driveway. The assistant had the horses already bridled and waiting — which he was instructed to do without saying a word to Archie. They mounted and rode off into the night under the light of a full moon.

∽

CHAPTER TWENTY-TWO

A CASE OF MISTAKEN

IDENTITY

*O*nny's journey to Rome was uneventful, with every detail of Apphia's scheme falling into place as she'd anticipated. The only time Onny was questioned about his social status was upon entering the house-prison complex.

The Roman guard demanded his identification papers, as well as wanting to know his purpose for visiting Paul, the incarcerated Christian missionary. Onny handed over the documentation Apphia's assistant had given him. He remembered receiving the following instructions: "*If and when you are asked for proof of identity or a certificate of leave, give them this document. This one with the Kyrios' seal is your certificate of leave and permission to travel. The other document is a letter that you must to give to Paul himself, when you meet him.*"

As far as Onny knew, the purpose of his visit was simple — to deliver a personal letter from his Kyrios' wife and to wait for Paul's reply. This was his first direct encounter with a Roman soldier, and he nervously stuttered through his explanation. Once his certificate of leave and permission to travel had been authenticated, he was granted entry into the house where Paul was kept under guard.

Escorted into a larger room, Onny found himself before Paul and his companions — Tychicus, Aristarchus, and Luke, Paul's physician — who cared for him. Several lamps illuminated the space, their warm glow mingling with the soft light filtering through a nearby window.

Paul, though not possessing the best eyesight, immediately noted something striking — the uncanny resemblance between this young messenger and his dear friend Philemon. He opened his mouth to speak, but the words did not come. In that very moment, the Holy Spirit restrained him. Instead, he simply offered a welcoming gesture, studying Onny's features with quiet intrigue.

Bowing low before Paul, Onny stammered, "G-G-Greetings to you, s-s-sir, from my K-K-Kyrios' wife, Apphia." With trembling hands, he presented the letter. One of Paul's attendants stepped forward, offering refreshments and setting a basin of water before him to wash his feet, along with a separate towel for his face.

Paul repositioned himself closer to the lamplight, carefully unfolding the letter. Before reading, he stole another glance at Onny, still taken aback by the young man's remarkable likeness to Philemon. "*Why does he look like both Philemon and Archie?*" *he thought to himself.*

As his eyes returned to the handwriting on the parchment, Paul paused again, the question still lingering in his mind. He read the entire letter silently. After finishing, he rolled it up and sat with his eyes closed.

At first, Onny thought Paul had fallen asleep, but after several moments, he noticed a slight shift in Paul's posture. Then, without a word, Paul unfolded the letter once more and began re-reading. Onny was intrigued. What was in this letter that Apphia had entrusted to him? Why was it so important?

Halfway through his second reading, Paul looked up and motioned for Onny to bring his seat closer. Onny obeyed and sat down, waiting for Paul to speak, but the apostle remained silent. It seemed as though Paul was also waiting ... but for what? Onny looked at him intently, unsure of what to expect.

Later, Paul would explain that he had been waiting for the Holy Spirit to give him the right words. At long last, he began. "Onesimus, it is a pleasure to meet you. And thank you for risking your life to bring me this letter from Apphia. Tell me, son, do you know what this letter is about?"

"N-n-no sir. I w-w-was not told anything. E-e-except to hand it t-t-to you in p-p-person," Onny stuttered, keeping his eyes down out of respect.

With a warm but cheeky smile, Paul responded, "It's okay, Onesimus. When you're with me — with us — you are permitted to make eye contact. So look at me, please."

Hesitantly, Onny lifted his gaze to Paul's gentle expression.

"Do you mean to say," Paul continued, "that you carried this letter all the way from Laodicea to Rome, and you weren't even tempted once to read it?"

Feeling a bit embarrassed, Onny looked down momentarily, then back at Paul. "Even if-f-f I w-w-was tempted, s-s-sir ..." he paused. "I don't ... I ... c-c-can't read!"

Paul laughed, and to his surprise, so did Onny. The awkwardness faded just a little. Reaching out and placing a hand on Onny's shoulder, Paul declared, "Well, Onesimus, I must agree with your Kyrios' wife — you are indeed a very trustworthy slave!"

"Th-th-thank you, sir, but my master calls me useless, even though I t-t-try my b-b-best. He's always called me that for as long as I can remember."

Paul's expression softened. "I can see that you do try hard, Onesimus," he replied. "By the way, what would you prefer to be called? Do you go by Onesimus or ...?"

"Oh, Onny sir!" Onny interjected with a smile. "Onny ... that's w-w-what my b-brother Aegie calls me!"

Paul glanced at his companions, who were only half paying attention to the conversation. Then, raising an eyebrow ... his voice increased slightly, he declared, "Right then, we'll call you Onny too!"

Turning back to Onny, Paul leaned in and asked, "Onny, are you at all curious about what your Kyrios' wife has written in this letter? What do you think?"

"I-I-I'm not sure, sir. I think it's p-p-private," Onny replied.

"You're right, Onny ... and by the way, you can call me Paul," he said with a grin. "Yes, it is private — because it's all about you!" Paul sat back and let that truth settle in.

After a moment Onny spoke. "Me?!" Onny blurted out. "Oh, that c-c-can't be, sir ... I mean, P-P-Paul. I'm not w-w-worthy for anyone writing ab-b-out!"

Reassuringly, Paul said, "Ah, but that's where you're wrong, Onny. Your Despoina, Apphia thinks you are worth writing about. She doesn't believe you are useless or worthless. That's why she chose you for this secret mission all the way to Rome! She thinks highly of you — and of your brother Archie ... I mean, Aegie, as you call him. It's all in here! Would you like me to read it to you?"

Still trying to process what Paul had just said, Onny hesitated. Then, looking up at Paul with wide eyes and a higher tone in his voice, he said, "Yes, p-p-please!"

Paul smiled. "Alright. Now, before we start, could you please pass me a cup of water? I'm a bit thirsty."

Onny stood and turned around, his eyes adjusting to the dim, dust-filled room. Tiny particles floated in the beams of light filtering through the window, shimmering in the still air. As he stepped toward the table where the water jug and cups were set, he reached out for the jug — only to accidentally knock over the cup.

He froze. "*What will Paul say now about my usefulness?*" the thought flashed through his mind.

But Paul and the others remained silent, as if they hadn't even noticed. No scolding, no reprimand. Just silence.

Quickly, Onny picked up the cup, poured some water into it, and brought it to Paul. "I-i-is there anything else I c-c-can get you, P-P-Paul, before you b-b-begin to read?" he asked hesitantly.

Paul smiled. "Thank you Onny, for asking. I'm all good for the moment. Now, son, as I read, I want you to stop me if there's something you don't understand or anything you want to ask me about. Okay?"

Onny nodded.

Slowly yet expressively, Paul began reading out loud. Onny listened intently, his heart pounding. Then, at the first mention of Master Dolion being his father, he bolted upright — his entire body trembling in shock.

"**STOP! STOP!** This c-c-cannot be t-t-true. It's a lie! I've n-n-never heard of this b-b-before. It can't be t-t-true!" His voice cracked with emotion. Then, as his breath slowed, he looked at Paul, eyes filled with desperation. "Can it, P-P-Paul?"

Out of respect for their new friend, Paul and the others who had been listening remained silent for several moments, allowing the weight of the revelation to settle upon the soft-hearted young slave.

Onny's chest rose and fell with uneven breaths. His mind raced, trying to make sense of what he had just heard. The quietness in the room felt heavy, like the dampness in the air, yet strangely comforting — not one of those present rushed to fill that space with empty words.

At last, Paul spoke gently. "Onny, I know this is a lot to take in. But I promise you, what is written here wasn't meant to harm you — it was meant to reveal the truth. And as Jesus says, '*The truth will set you free.*'"

Onny let out a bitter laugh. "That's easy for you to s-s-say ... You've always b-b-been a free m-m-man, Paul ... even though now you are in p-p-prison! How can the t-t-truth set me free? Can y-you tell me that — p-p-please?!"

Paul didn't react to Onny's outburst of frustration. He simply waited, then spoke in a steady, calm voice.

"Onny, I'm not talking about chains or walls, or the kind of freedom men give and take away. Jesus speaks of a different kind of freedom — the kind that lives in your heart and mind."

Onny hesitated. He opened his mouth as if to speak, but no words came.

Paul waited, then asked softly, "Are you ready for me to continue reading, son?"

Onny gave a slow nod and settled back into his chair.

෴

Contemplations for Individual Reflection and Group Discussion

CHAPTER #21 & #22:

- Have you ever experienced the disappearance of a close friend or family member? (including a pet) What did you do?
- For the safety of another person, have you ever withheld knowledge of an incident or situation?
- How do you discern the right time to write that letter or make that call?
- What was it like to hear a hidden truth / fact about yourself for the first time?

CHAPTER TWENTY-THREE

CONFRONTING

TRUTH

*P*aul picked up where he had left off, reading steadily until he came to the part where Apphia wrote about how much Onny resembled his Kyrios, Philemon.

"WAIT!" Onny stood up again, his voice rising with urgency. "Are y-y-you saying that n-n-not only was Master D-D-Dolion my father, b-b-but that M-M-Master Phil is my brother too? But Aegie is m-m-my brother!" His stuttering seemed to hinder his speech, but not his thoughts.

His mind was reeling. None of this made sense.

"This is t-t-too hard for me to under-s-s-stand, P-Paul! How can K-K-Kyrios Dolion be my f-f-father? My E-E-Emaye and Abaye raised me!"

Paul reached out and took Onny's trembling hand, coaxing him gently back into his seat. Holding his gaze, he spoke plainly.

"The letter explains that Philemon's father took advantage of his position as master, lured your mother into his bed, and had sexual relations with her. She became pregnant and after nine months, gave birth to you."

Paul paused, allowing the weight of his words to settle. Then, with warmth in his voice, he added: "So, Onny, it seems that you actually have two brothers ... Aegie and Philemon."

Onny pulled away from Paul's touch. This time, he was more angry than shocked. "B-b-but he hates me! He detests m-m-me! He thinks I'm useless … I've heard him s-s-say it hundreds of times! Why would he hate me so m-m-much, Paul?"

Paul waited, allowing time for Onny's frustration to settle just a little before speaking again. Then, in a calm and thoughtful tone, he said, "Maybe, my son, it's not that he hates *you* so much … but more that he hates what his father did to your mother. And maybe — just maybe he doesn't know how to handle it. The truth is, you are after all, both his slave and his brother. Maybe, Onny, *that's* what he really hates."

Paul left those words hang in the air, giving Onny space in order to process them.

Suddenly, a deep, guttural wail burst from Onny's throat. *"Oh—ah—uh!"* The sound of his grief filled the room, raw and unrestrained. It went on and on, his body shaking with sobs that had been buried for far too long.

Paul sat with him, not interrupting, allowing the young man to release the pain he had carried for years.

At last, when Onny's cries began to soften, Paul spoke again, his voice warm and steady. "What is it, Onny?"

Onny wiped his eyes and took a shaky breath. "S-s-so, I had t-t-two fathers ... but I have n-n-no father." His voice cracked under the weight of his words. "The m-m-man who was my b-b-birth father died when I was a b-b-baby — I never knew him. And the f-f-father who raised me as his own ... I can b-b-barely remember him. All I remember is how much it hurt when he d-d-died."

He hesitated, then added, "K-K-Kyrios Phil said my Abaye died of a b-b-broken heart. D-d-do you think that's t-t-true, Paul?"

Paul's expression softened. In a reassuring tone, he replied, "Onny, I believe it's very possible. Yes ... I believe it is."

He paused for a moment, then continued, "It seems to me that you are in desperate need of a father's love and acceptance. And though we have only just met, let me offer you something to consider. You are welcome to stay here as long as you need ... and if you're willing, I would be honoured to call you my adopted son. I will accept you as you are. I will love you for who you are, Onny. If you'll have me ... I would gladly be your father."

Without hesitation, Onny leapt from his seat and wrapped his long, gentle arms around Paul's chest. Sobbing, he whispered, "But you d-d-don't even know m-m-me!"

Paul held him close and whispered back, "Maybe I don't ... but Onny, I know your heart, son. And I want to help you understand how you can also know the heart of God — your true Father in heaven. He loves you more than I ever could."

Onny pulled away, his eyes widening with realization. "I'd like that v-v-very much ... b-b-but my Despoina has instructed me to w-w-wait for your letter of re-p-p-ply," he said.

Paul grinned. "Oh, there's no rush, son! I'll get around to writing back when the time is right."

Onny hesitated, then asked enthusiastically, "W-w-well, in that c-c-case ... can I c-c-call you Abaye?"

Paul reeled back in laughter. "Of course you can!" Then, turning to his companions, he announced, "Let's celebrate our newest family member, boys!"

He turned back to Onny, holding up the letter and speaking in a reassuring tone. "Onny, my son ... we'll talk more about this later, hmm?"

Onny nodded, beaming. "Y-y-yes, Abaye, I'd I-like that."

ᔕ

CHAPTER TWENTY-FOUR

WHAT'S IN A NAME?

*J*he time Onny spent serving Paul in his new home — albeit temporary — moved along seamlessly. Days quickly turned into weeks, weeks into months, and before long, more than a year had passed since Onny arrived in Rome and was adopted by Paul. Onny cared for Paul with loving respect and compassion. While Luke served as Paul's physician, Onny had become his personal carer.

Since Onny's arrival at the house-prison, he had seen many people come and go. Some stayed for only an hour or two, others overnight, and some for a week or more. At various times, several of Paul's companions departed on mission assignments given under the Lord's direction.

These were exciting days, with visitors from all walks of life — rich and poor seeking guidance ... sick people in need of healing ... Romans, Jewish leaders, Greeks, and people of other nationalities. To Onny's surprise, some were even from Africa.

Onny not only cared for Paul's personal needs but also cleaned, swept, and washed dishes and clothing. He was keen to serve in any way he could. He was allowed to come and go freely, delivering messages to people outside the house-prison. Whenever he was sent out as a messenger, Paul or one of the others ensured he carried his identity documents with him for his safety.

Every day was a learning experience for Onny, keeping him busy with a variety of tasks. With each new day, a stronger bond formed between Paul and his young, adopted slave-son. And with Onny bearing such a strong resemblance to Philemon, it was a double blessing for Paul.

❧

In the days, weeks, and months following Onny's arrival, the Apostle gently ministered God's grace to the young slave. Led by the Holy Spirit, Paul sensed that the time had come to help Onny more fully understand who he was and what his name meant. He also reminded Onny that his birth father was the one who had given him his name.

The Holy Spirit revealed to Paul that Onny had always struggled to grasp the connection between the significance of his name and his true identity. When Paul discerned the time was right, he asked, "Tell me, Onny — what do you know about your name? What have you been told about it? What does it mean to you?"

"M-m-my name is Onny," he replied. "That's all I kn-know. I've al-w-ways been c-c-called Onny ever s-s-since I can remember!"

Paul gently pressed him a bit further, "There must be something more, my son?!"

With some agitation creeping into his voice. "No, Abaye! Th-th-that's all. I d-d-don't know! I'm just s-s-stupid and useless!" Onny replied.

Paul realised he needed to back off a little and allow Onny time to think and breathe. "May I have a cup of water please Onny?" This diversion enabled Onny to regain his focus. Then turning to Tychicus, he asked him to write two Greek words on the dusty floor:

$$\Sigma IICHR\mathcal{E}ST\acute{\Omega}S \dots \text{ and } \dots \Lambda CHR\mathcal{E}ST\acute{\Omega}S.$$

As Tychicus scribbled out the words on the floor, Onny watched on with intrigue.

"Onny, have a look at what Tychicus has scribbled here. These are two different words, see?" Paul instructed.

Taken aback, Onny was quick to remind Paul and the others that he could neither read nor write.

"Well, my son" Paul declared with a chuckle. "I think that's about to change, and there's no time like the present to start! So let's begin your first reading lesson, shall we?

"Tychicus has written two words. One means 'useless,' and the other means 'useful.' Take a close look at both and tell me what you see, Onny."

Onny was about to protest again about being illiterate when Tychicus piped up, "Let me help you Onny! Paul asked you '*what you see*' ... not what you can read!"

Taking that comment to heart, and a deep breath, Onny stooped down and studied the scribbly lines and shapes on the floor. At last, he looked up and announced, "They look almost the same, but they are different there!" He pointed to the beginning of each of the words.

"Yay! Go you!" everyone in the room cheered loudly.

"Well done, Onny!" Paul said. "You should be very proud of yourself — that's an amazing observation." He paused, then became serious again. "Now ... let's have a closer look, hey?!"

Feeling rather chuffed at this major achievement, Onny asked, "Ok-k-kay, but how d-d-do we do that?"

Paul explained, "Now, remember what I said about the two words. One means ...?"

"Use-f-f-ful?" Onny said hesitantly.

"Well done, Onny! And what does the other word mean?" Paul asked.

"The other w-w-word means 'useless' ... j-j-just like me," he replied disparagingly, his tone laced with an edge of sadness.

Appearing to ignore Onny's last remark, Paul said, "Onny, I want you to smudge out the parts of the words that look the same. Can you do that?"

"I th-think I can," Onny responded.

Tychicus helped him identify and wipe out the '*chrestos*' part of each word.

"Thanks, T-T-Tychie, for your help!" Onny said as he looked back at Paul.

"That's great, Onny. You're doing well son," Paul said with encouragement. "Now, let's have a look at what's left."

Using his walking stick to point, Paul explained, "Okay, look. Here we have 'eu,' and over here we have 'a.'"

Copying exactly what Paul had just done, Onny leaned over and pointed with his finger. "'Eu' and 'a' ... o-k-k-kay ... but wh-wh-at do they mean, Abaye?"

"That's a great question, Onny! You're such a fast learner!" Paul said with a smile. "One means 'good — on the inside', and the other means 'not so good — or lacking — on the outside.'"

"Oh, I g-g-get it! Kinda like our b-b-belly button — 'innie' and 'outie'?" Onny blurted out.

Everyone in the room cracked up laughing, bringing some much-needed relief to the tension Onny obviously had been feeling up to that moment.

Regaining his composure, Paul asked, "Now, it's important for us to understand the part of the word that Tychicus just wiped out. Tychie, write the word again please — just once this time ... if you will."

Tychicus wrote in bigger letters: 'chrestos'.

"Thanks Tychie," Paul said. Turning to Onny, he continued. "Now, Onny, I want you to understand what this word 'chrestos' actually means. Are you with me, son?"

Onny nodded ... even though he was not quite sure of where this was all going.

Paul continued, "This word 'chrestos' means 'useful' or 'beneficial.' Now it's your turn, Onny. Can you tell me — what does 'chrestos' mean?"

Onny hesitated, then replied, "Hmm ... C-c-'chrestos' means ... 'usef-f-ful' or 'benif-f-icial'? I th-think?"

Paul smiled and reached out to give him a fist bump. Onny was beaming with pride — after all this time, he was actually learning to read!

Paul continued, "Great! Now let's look at putting the 'a' in front of 'chrestos' ... to make the word ...?" He waited for Onny to pick up on the clue.

"That's 'achr-chr-chrestos'!" Onny exclaimed.

"Right again!" Paul continued. "Remember, 'a' means 'not so good — on the outside.' So Onny, what do you think 'achrestos' means? Hmm?"

Again, Onny hesitated, his voice laced with uncertainty. "I th-think 'achr-chr-chrestos' means ... 'not g-g-good — on the outside!' No! W-w-wait!" He straightened up. His confidence growing. "I th-think it means ... 'not good at b-b-being useful'!"

Paul leaned back and grinned with delight. "You're doing really great, Onny! We're nearly done ... just a little bit more, hey?!"

Onny sat taller, and moved in closer with a deep sense of achievement settling within him.

"Now, if 'achrestos' means 'not good at being useful,' as you say, then when we put 'eu' in front of 'chrestos,' we get the opposite, right? Remember, 'eu' means 'good — on the inside,' and 'chrestos' means ..." Paul paused, waiting.

"**Useful**!" Onny shouted.

"Great work!" Paul acknowledged with another fist bump. "So, what do you think 'euchrestos' means ... hmm?"

Onny took his time in considering his answer. He spoke softly, as if reasoning with himself — slowly, with a hint of wonder but also a growing sense of confidence.

"W-w-well, if 'achrestos' means 'not good at b-being useful,' then I f-figure that 'eu-euchrestos' would mean something like … 'on the inside, I'm g-g-ood at b-b-being useful?!'"

The room erupted. Hands flew into the air, cheers filled the space, and Onny, though puzzled at first, found himself smiling and joining in the excitement.

Paul urged him, "Say it again."

Onny hesitated, then repeated, "On the inside … I'm g-good at b-being useful!" This time a charged silence filled the room.

"Say it again, son. But this time — stand up and say it louder."

Onny stood to his feet, inhaled deeply, and declared, **"On the inside … I'm good at being useful!"** He paused, as if truly hearing himself for the first time. Then with a newfound conviction, he spoke even more loudly, **"On the inside … I'm good at being useful!"**

The room exploded as grown men were jumping about like little kids with ecstatic applause and hugs all around.

Paul embraced Onny tightly. "Listen to yourself, Onesimus, my son ... whose name means 'useful.' Listen to what you just said about yourself!"

Onny froze. In that moment, he realized — he had actually '*heard*' his real name for the first time in his life.

Closing his eyes, he stood before the others, overcome with emotion. A quiet sob escaped him as he whispered, "I am Onesimus. On the inside of me ... I am useful." To everyone's amazement, this was the first time they'd heard him speak without stuttering.

Then he lifted his head, his voice steady and full of confidence, he declared: **"I am Onesimus. My name means useful. I am not useless — I am useful!"**

He opened his eyes, then without hesitation, threw his arms around Tychicus and Paul. The others rushed in, wrapping him in a group embrace.

For the first time ever, Onesimus felt something he had never known before — a profound sense of worth. From that time on, 'the truth' that Paul had spoken of earlier, gradually began settling deep into his soul. He felt free. With each new day, he wondered to himself, "Could it get any better than this?"

❦

Contemplations for Individual Reflection and Group Discussion

CHAPTER #23:

- Do you know anyone who has actually died of a broken heart?
- Can you recall the first time you experienced unconditional love?

CHAPTER #24:

- Have you ever researched the meaning of your name? What does it mean? Are there any contradictions to your character or personality?
- When was the last time / first time that someone actually sat you down and gently explained something that was difficult to understand?
- Have you ever had an actual 'light bulb' moment that changed your life? What was it like for you?

CHAPTER TWENTY-FIVE

NEW NAME

AND NEW PURPOSE

$\mathscr{F}$rom that day on, Onny requested that everyone use his proper name, embracing the truth of what it meant.

Enthused with a new purpose, Onesimus devotedly undertook many tasks that had been neglected in Paul's house of confinement. He cleaned, dusted, de-cobwebbed, and rearranged furniture, in addition to cooking and washing — all without a single spill, drop, or breakage. In fact, the energy and fervour he displayed as he continued to wait on Paul and his friends, including visitors, began to affect them. Not only did they feel exhausted just watching him, but they also began to feel almost useless in comparison. Eventually, they had to ask him to slow down!

He also delivered messages from Paul to people within the city precincts and bought food from the market. Having a certificate of leave, meant that he was free to come and go from the house.

The longer he stayed, the closer between him and Paul grew. His life had radically changed since arriving in Rome and meeting Paul. He had never felt so happy and settled.

As Paul observed the dramatic change in Onny's mindset and behaviour — including his speech, which was less stuttery — the Holy Spirit began to impress on his heart, that it time to introduce Onesimus to Jesus. Up until this time, Paul and his friends had simply loved on this young slave and showered him with encouragement and affirmation.

One morning just as Onny was about to sweep the floor, the time seemed right for Paul to revisit the meaning on Onny's name. Paul insisted that Onny stop ... leave the dust and sit next to him. And just like previously, Paul asked one of the others to write on the floor the words 'euchrestos' and 'achrestos'.

Paul nudged Onny to respond. Without hesitation Onny said, "This is me!" as he drew a circle around the word 'euchrestos', and then proceeded to wipe out 'achrestos'. "I am useful. My n-name means 'useful'. I am n-n-not useless — I am Onesimus!" he said with his chest puffed out and his head held proudly.

"That's great, Onesimus and so very true!" said Paul with a smile; but then he gestured for Onny to follow him. Curious, Onny obeyed. Paul led him to a small polished bronze mirror resting against the wall. "Now, I want you to have a good look at yourself in the mirror, Onesimus."

Onny hesitated, then peered into the reflective surface. He gasped. He hardly recognized himself! His face, once downcast, now radiated joy. His posture was straight, his eyes alive with purpose. "I look ... s-so d-different! I f-feel d-different!" he murmured softly.

Paul nodded. "Yes, my son. That's because you *are* different." Paul affirmed. "The outside looks different because the inside has changed. You are seeing what we have always seen in you. Now, do you see it too?"

Onny swallowed hard and nodded. "Yes, Abaye. I see!"

Then Paul turned and asked Timothy to scribble down two more words:

$$\Sigma IICHRIS\mathcal{T}\Omega S \ldots \text{ and } \ldots \Lambda CHR\bar{I}S\mathcal{T}\Omega S$$

Paul instructed, "Now, have a good look at these two words Onesimus. What do you notice?"

Onny examined them carefully and answered, "Wow! They look almost the same as the other words ... but they are different! What d-d-do they mean Abaye?"

"Good observation, my son. And an even better question!" said Paul, as he continued to wait on the Holy Spirit.

Onny impatiently repeated, "*B-b-but what d-d-do they mean Abaye, p-p-please?*"

"Remember the 'Λ *(α)* ' from the other word? What did it mean?" asked Paul.

"Oh, I n-know! It means 'outside' or 'not g-good' ... I think!" replied Onny.

"Okay. And what about the 'ΣII *(εν)* '?" enquired Paul.

166

Like a very willing student bouncing up and down in his seat Onny raised his hand. "I n-know! I know!" he beamed.

Paul nodded, "Well ... ?"

"The '$\Sigma\Pi$' m-means ' inside' or 'g-good' right?!" Onny said.

"Well done Onesimus. Now, will you please wipe out the first letter 'Λ'? Then have a look at what's left," Paul continued. Onny did as he was instructed.

"Now son, the letters you see that are remaining spell the word Christos or Christ — which means 'the annointed one.'"

"Oh, is th-that who you t-talk about when you are telling others ab-bout Jesus Christ?" asked Onny.

"That's right, my son. Good observation," Paul explained. "When you hear me talk to both Gentiles and Jews about Jesus, I mostly refer to him as 'Jesus the Christ' — in Greek it is 'Iesous Kristos' or 'Yeshua Mashiach' in Hebrew."

"Yes Abaye, I have heard you use b-b-both ways when talking about J-Jesus. But w-what does 'annointed' mean Abaye ... and w-w-what does this have to do with me?" asked Onny.

"What a curious question Onesimus! I'm getting to that!" Paul answered. "So, as we know, the 'Λ' means outside. And we also know that '$CHR\bar{I}ST\Omega S$' means 'Christ the annointed one'. When we read *ΛCHRĪSTŌS*, we are actually referring to someone who is outside of Christ, or to put it another way ... someone who does not belong to Christ."

Onny seemed puzzled. "When you s-s-say ... 'someone who does not belong to C-Christ', does that m-m-mean ... they are f-free because they do not belong to Christ ... like a slave would belong to their master? I'm a b-b-bit con...fused!"

"Wow, Onesimus! You ask the most probing questions!" replied Paul. "Firstly, we need to back up a bit and take this carefully and slowly. If you can understand this then it will change your life forever!" he explained.

Continuing on, he said, "So, as we know, the '*Λ*' means outside. It also means not good or not worthwhile. Therefore to be outside of Christ ... is neither good nor worthwhile."

Paul closed his eyes momentarily. Onny could tell that he was praying quietly. Then he opened his eyes widely and smiled, yet he spoke in a serious tone. "Let me talk to Onny the slave. I believe the Lord wants to remind you that you had no choice in being a slave. Right? You were born into slavery." Onny nodded with intrigue.

"Right!" he continued, "And, when your brother Aegie was offered his freedom by Kyrios Phil, what did he do?"

Onny jumped about partly excitedly but partly with curiosity, "He ch-ch-chose to accept the offer! But I s…still don't g-g-get it. What does this h-h-have to do with w-w-what we were t-t-talking about, Abaye?"

"It has everything to do with it Onny, my son!" Paul declared. "Anyone who is outside of Christ is a slave to sin. Accepting Jesus Christ as Lord and Saviour, is really accepting your freedom from being a slave to sin. Jesus died for our sins to set us free from the bondage of sin and death. Anyone who accepts Christ's offer of salvation is 'in Christ … 'euchristos'! And let me tell you Onesimus, from my own experience … to be 'in Christ … 'euchristos' … that's a really good thing!"

Paul took a breath and waited. He could tell Onny was taking all this in. Then he explained, "Onny, to be 'in Christ' (euchristos) is to be useful, filled with purpose, and connected to Christ. In contrast, being 'outside of Christ' (achristos) is like being useless, without purpose, and separated from Christ."

Onny continued to soak in what Paul was explaining, then all of a sudden he burst out saying, "Thank you! Thank you, Abaye for explaining all this. It's a lot to t-take in … but you have reminded m-me of when I s-started learning how to r-read, the difference it made in m-my life to realise for the first time, that I was euchrestos

— useful! I remember the d-difference it made to me then, and now! Look at me! I'm less clumsy ... and I hardly s-stutter at all!"

He took another deep breath, and was about to continue when Paul interjected. "Onesimus, my son. Where do you think you would like to be from now on — in Christ's family or outside?"

With much joy and enthusiasm, Onny replied, "Oh Abaye, because I have heard you talk to so many people about Jesus, and His forgiveness ... I know that I w-want to be p-part of His family. I want to be 'eu...christos'!"

Paul maintained his composure as he said, "That's great news Onesimus! And just so that you know — when you are euchristos ... you are even more euchrestos!"

"How c-can that b-be Abaye? I know I-I-I am euchrestos!" Onny enquired naïvely.

"Because ..." Paul went on to explain, "You now have the Holy Spirit living in you to empower you to be the best version of Onesimus that you can be!" Paul waited before adding, "Come. Let's go back to the brass mirror. Have a deep look into the mirror and tell me what you see."

Paul stood beside Onny as he looked into the dimmed reflection of his face. Taking his time, he stared hard, his reflection slowly coming into focus. He saw not just his face but his identity in

Christ — a new creation. After a few moments, he turned to Paul and the others and declared: "Wh…en I look deeply into the mirror, I no longer see a slave who is useless and bound. I see a young man who is a child of God. I am 'eu…christos'. I am in Christ! I see Onesimus who is em…powered by the Holy Spirit … to be 'euchrestos' in every…thing that I do and s…ay!"

Everyone in the room clapped for joy as tears soaked their bearded faces.

Paul added one more thought to Onny's declaration of faith. "This is most wonderful news, Onesimus my son. You have just reminded me of something in what you have just declared.

"What is th-that Abaye?" Onny enquired.

"A few years ago I wrote a letter to the church in Corinth to encourage them" Paul said. "I wrote something like this: '*so that if anyone is in Christ — that person is a new creature; the old things have passed away. Lo and behold, all things have become new.*' Or to put it even more simply: '*whoever is a believer in Christ is a new creation. The old way of living has disappeared. A new way of living has come into existence.*'"

From that moment, Onny never once stuttered again. His newfound faith filled him with much joy ... which spontaneously poured out of his heart and turned into singing. The first time he sang, all the others were moved to tears, as the words flawlessly flowed out of his mouth ... His beautiful tenor voice filling the room. The song he sang over and over went something like:

'Who the Son sets free
Oh, is free indeed
I'm a child of God, yes, I am.

Free at last, He has ransomed me
His grace runs deep
While I was a slave to sin, Jesus died for me
Yes, He died for me.

Who the Son sets free
Oh, is free indeed
I'm a child of God, yes, I am.'

As he grew in his faith, he boldly shared with everyone he came in contact with that he no longer felt like a useless slave in his heart — even though he was still legally a slave to Philemon.

⤿

Contemplations for Individual Reflection and Group Discussion

CHAPTER #25:

- Take up the challenge of looking deep into the mirror and documenting what / who you see. Ask the Holy Spirit to open your eyes and your ears ... wait for Him to speak to you.

- Is there a particular song that captures or expresses the state of your heart? Or one that you can identify as being significant in your spiritual growth?

CHAPTER TWENTY-SIX

HIS WILL ...

IN HIS WAY ...

IN HIS TIME

Circa AD 60

175

*B*ack in Laodicea meanwhile, life went on as usual, despite the fact that Archie (aka Aegie) missed his brother terribly. After about a year or so, the consensus among the other slaves and staff was that Onny had either stolen money and run away or had likely met with foul play.

Not once, however had Paul questioned Onny about how he had acquired the money he carried with him. However, it was generally assumed that he had stolen it, as Apphia's letter to Paul made no mention of any money. Paul simply believed that the truth about the money would be revealed in due time.

It had been just over a year since Paul and Onny had bonded. Paul sought the Lord's plan and purpose for each new day. One morning, the Spirit prompted him to raise the important matter of returning home. He was fully aware of the risks involved for his adopted son. Firstly, Onny's certificate of leave was just that — a temporary leave, not a certificate of freedom — so it would certainly have an expiration date. Secondly, and more seriously, if Onny had indeed stolen from his master, he could face severe punishment or even execution.

Paul asked Onny to sit with him and spoke gently, informing him that the time had come for him to return to his Kyrios and his brother. He reminded him that Apphia was still waiting for a reply to her letter and that the Lord had spoken to him, making it clear that now was the time to respond.

Onny was surprised by this news. Though he loved being with Paul and had gained confidence through his newfound faith, he expressed his uneasiness about what might happen to him when he returned. However, his relationship with Paul was secure, and his trust in the Lord was strong.

As it turned out, Paul had already written a lengthy letter to the church in Colossae and had asked Tychicus to deliver it. With tears welling, Paul commissioned Onesimus to accompany Tychicus. He also explained that he had written a short letter to Philemon rather than to Apphia. "As Philemon is your Kyrios, it is only right that I address him on your behalf," he explained.

Supplies were gathered — enough for at least the first leg of the journey. Neither Paul nor Onesimus slept well that night, as the anticipation of grief in saying goodbye was intense. Both tossed and turned, wondering what the future might hold.

The next morning, after an early breakfast, Onesimus and Tychicus bid farewell to Paul and the others. The close-knit group huddled together as Paul prayed for the Lord's blessing and protection over them.

In their final embrace, there were many tears — especially from Paul and Onny — uncertain if they would ever see each other again. Paul whispered reassuringly, "My son, you have my heart, and I have yours." He pulled back slightly so they were face to face. "Remember how I told you about King Solomon? He once wrote to his own son: 'Trust in the Lord with all your heart. In everything you do and say, put Him first, and He will make clear the way you are to go.' Onesimus, do not worry about Philemon at all. It is more important to trust in the Lord's will, in His way, and in His time."

Onny quietly responded, "Thank you, Abaye. Thank you ... for everything! You accepted me just as I was. You taught me to read. You encouraged me to believe in myself as a useful person. You introduced me to Jesus. I love you, and I take your heart with me back to my home and family."

಄

CHAPTER TWENTY-SEVEN

THE TRUTH

BE TOLD

*T*heir special mission to deliver letters to Colossae and Laodicea was largely without incident, apart from the times they had opportunities to share about their faith in Jesus.

With Epaphras ministering to Paul in prison, Tychicus and Onny were received with open arms by the elders and the whole church in Colossae. They shared the latest news about Paul — his health, well-being, and future missionary plans. Tychicus had also been instructed by Paul to gather as many details as possible about the Colossian church's circumstances.

The Colossian Christians were pleased to hear about Onny's newfound faith and his well-being, as news had already spread from Laodicea about his disappearance. On behalf of Onny, Tychicus requested that the Colossians ensure his safety by not sending any word ahead to Laodicea.

After a few days of being treated as special guests in Colossae, the two departed for Laodicea — the last leg of their epistle deliveries. They were sent on their way with the Lord's blessing from the Colossian church.

Onny talked non-stop as he made full use of his release from his speech impediment. Tychicus listened as Onny shared both his excitement and anticipation of returning home, as well as his anxieties of what might happen to him. Tychicus prayed in the Spirit the whole time.

Eventually, they rounded a bend in the road, on the crest of a hill from where they could see the oikos estate where he'd grown up. Tychicus stopped and asked Onesimus to kneel down with him in the middle of the road before the Lord. They gave thanks for His protection and provision. They acknowledged the Lord's faithfulness and purpose in everything that had occurred over the past year and a bit. Tychicus especially prayed for the Lord's favour over Onesimus, and for Philemon to receive him back with grace and mercy.

Walking through the gate of the estate, brought back an assortment of different thoughts — happy and painful memories filling Onesimus with a range of mixed emotions. But despite these internal distractions, he walked confidently beside his companion. At the first sighting of the 'runaway slave', news spread like wildfire.

They were greeted warmly at the door of the house by Apphia. The Lord had shown her that, in this matter, she needed to restrain herself from becoming emotionally engaged with the visitors. She was also shown that it was imperative for her to allow Philemon to handle the contents of the letter. She ushered the two men with their heads still covered into the sitting room, leaving them there while she went to find her husband.

"Phil, you have two unexpected visitors," she announced. "They have informed me they are here to deliver a personal letter from Paul to you."

Philemon entered the room, not knowing whom or what to expect. Tychicus and Onesimus both bowed before him in respect, still with their heads covered. Philemon greeted them formally and indicated that they could approach and hand over Paul's letter. Tychicus stood up and bowed as he approached and handed over the letter.

In an awkward moment of exchange, Philemon asked him his name. "Sir, we have not met before. It is an honour to meet you Philemon. My name is Tychicus. I am one of a small group of friends who have been ministering to Paul, in his prison-house in Rome for more than a year."

Philemon gave a quick sideways glance at Onesimus, who was nervously awaiting for the Kyrios to ask for *his* identity; but to his great relief, it seemed that Philemon was more interested in reading Paul's letter.

Philemon called one his servants to usher the two visitors into another waiting room for refreshments and foot washing, while he sat and read his letter in private. As they left the room walking backwards, they kept their heads bowed.

Phil was rather excited to hear from Paul after all this time, but he was totally unprepared for what he was about to read. Sitting down in his comfy chair, he unfolded the letter and began reading:

> This letter is from me, Paul. I am here in prison (under house arrest) in Rome because I serve Christ Jesus, and our dear brother Timothy is also with me.
>
> We are writing to you, Philemon, our beloved friend and fellow worker in Christ. We also send our greetings to Apphia, our sister in the faith, and to Archippus, our fellow soldier in the Lord. And we send greetings to the church that meets in your home.
>
> I pray that God our Father and the Lord Jesus Christ will continue to bless you with grace and fill your heart with peace.
>
> Philemon, whenever I pray for you, I always thank the Lord, remembering you with gratitude. I have heard of your love for all of God's people and your unwavering faith in the Lord Jesus. As we serve Christ together, I pray that your faith will grow even stronger and

that you will come to understand every good thing we share in Him. My friend, you continue to refresh the hearts of God's people with your love. Your kindness has brought me great joy and encouragement.

Now, I have a request to make of you. As one who belongs to Christ (and led you to Him), I could give you a direct command to do the right thing. But instead, because of love, I appeal to you. As an old man now and a prisoner for the sake of Christ Jesus, I'm asking you to show kindness to Onesimus — yes, you read that right, Onesimus!

More than a year ago, he showed up here unexpectedly. He has served me well while I've been in prison. In that time, I've come to love him as my own son, and I led him to faith in Jesus, and so now, in Christ, he has new life with God.

I know that for years, you may have considered him of little use to you — useless, to be more precise. But now he is useful to both of us. That is why I am sending him back to you, and with him, my very heart. I would have preferred to keep him here with me, so he could serve me on your behalf while I am in chains for the gospel. But I did not want to act without your consent. Any kindness you show to him should be given willingly, not out of obligation.

Perhaps this separation happened so that you could now have him back forever — not just as a slave, but as something far greater. He is not only a beloved brother in Christ but a brother to you in every way. Onesimus has become very dear to me, but he is even more so to you — both as a brother in the flesh and in the Lord.

So if you consider me your partner in faith, welcome Onesimus as you would welcome me. If he has wronged you in any way or owes you anything, charge it to me. Yes, I will repay it! (I've written this with my own hand.) But let's not forget that you owe me your very life — remember when you said, "I owe you"? And of course, remember I was the one who brought you the good news of Christ!

My dear brother, I want you to know that you
will refresh my heart in the Lord by doing this.
I am confident in your obedience, knowing
that you will do even more than I ask.

Oh, and one more thing — please prepare a
guest room for me, for I trust that through
your prayers, in His time ... God will allow me to
visit you soon.

Oh, by the way, Epaphras — whom you know
well — is also now my fellow prisoner in Christ
Jesus. He sends his greetings, as do Mark,
Aristarchus, Demas, and Luke — my co-workers
in the faith.

May the grace of the Lord Jesus Christ, the love
of God our Father and the peace of the Holy
Spirit be with your spirit.

After he had finished reading, he sat motionless — deep in
thought. His heart and mind were in a quandary. After some time,
Apphie came to check on him, concerned by the prolonged silence.

"Apphie, as you already know, this is from Paul — I think you'd
better read it," he said, handing her the letter. She sat down beside

her husband and began to read. Phil remained still and silent, staring into space.

After she'd finished reading, Apphie placed the letter in-between them as she became a little fidgety. She hesitated before speaking. Clearing her throat, she began: "Ahem. Before you do or say anything Phil, I need to confess something to you."

She went on to explain the actions she had taken when Onesimus went missing.

At first, Phil was furious that she had acted on her own without consulting him or informing him afterward. He stomped about the room, ranting and raving.

"Sending my slave away! Taking my money! Concealing the fact that you knew anything at all! Writing to Paul and forging the manumission! How dare you! You've betrayed me, Apphie!"

After venting his anger at the top of his voice for several minutes, he paused to catch his breath. In that very moment, the Lord captured Phil's breath and touched his heart. With his heart pounding and his lungs gasping for air — he was reminded of the day that Paul had prayed for his life to be restored.

Instantly, he fell to his knees and wept uncontrollably as he realized the depth of God's grace and forgiveness. Paul *was* right — he did owe Paul his life! He recalled his own words, spoken before several witnesses after Paul had prayed for him and brought him back to life: *"I owe you!"*

Once again, Apphie knelt beside her husband, wrapping her arms around his trembling body as he broke down in sobs.

As the tide of his sobbing began to subside and the tremors of his adrenaline rush faded, Philemon stood to his feet. As he regained his composure, he turned to Apphie. "Bring in Tychicus and his companion please," he said. Though now, in his mind, there was no question as to who that companion was.

When they re-entered the room with their heads bowed, Apphie couldn't help but notice how Philemon stood tall, his expression completely unreadable — almost stoic and aloof.

Without hesitation, he addressed them. "Thank you for delivering Paul's letter today. I have read it carefully and given serious thought to my response."

Sensing the tension in the air, Onesimus could no longer contain himself. The apprehension was unbearable — he didn't know what to expect, but he feared the worst. He threw himself prostate to the floor. "Please Kyrios ... forgive me for everything. I know how much shame I have brought to you, and you have every reason to do whatever you have to, to your useless slave! But sir, I want you to know that my Abaye, Paul helped me to see that I am not useless — either as a slave or a person. The one who you always have called 'useless' is now a believer in the Lord Jesus Christ. I ask you to show mercy and …"

"Stop right there, Onesimus! Stop it!" (Only later did it dawn on them both that this was the first time Philemon had ever spoken Onny's real name).

Phil dropped to his knees in front of Onny. For the first time in both their lives, he touched his half-brother. Reaching out, he took Onny's hands, and lifted him up to his knees. Then, in a poignant moment of compassion and grace, Phil gently raised Onny's head to look into his face.

This was the first time either of them had ever looked each other in the eyes — a moment of undeniable truth for them both. It was as if they were gazing into a crystal-clear mirror, seeing a remarkable likeness of themselves — one that neither had ever recognised before. Onesimus looked like a younger Philemon, and Philemon … an older version of Onesimus.

Very quietly and gently, Phil spoke, tears streaming down his face. "Onesimus, it is I who need to ask for your forgiveness — for the countless times I labelled you 'useless,' for the hundreds of times I sniggered at you and laughed as you stumbled about while trying to fulfill your duties. And for every time I mocked you when you stuttered while speaking. I am so sorry for all of that and more."

Onny was speechless at what he was hearing. This was his brother speaking directly to him — with remorse and compassion. For those in the room, it was overwhelming to witness.

"I especially ask you, my brother, Onesimus, to forgive me for treating you with such contempt for who you are. I am sorry for blaming you and holding you responsible for the circumstances of your birth. Before my mitéra died, she tried to help me to come to terms with the fact that you had no choice or control over your coming into this world. Since then, I've had to work through a lot in forgiving my patéras — *our father* — for what he did to your Emaye and Abaye.

"And now, as I have come to understand, we are also brothers in our common faith in Jesus. Onesimus, can you find it in your heart to forgive me? Even if you cannot, I want you to know that from this day forward, I accept you as my 'adelphos' — my brother in life and in Christ Jesus. Let me put it in terms I believe you will appreciate. Onesimus ... you are *euchrestos* to me, both as my brother in life, and together we are now *euchristos*.

And of course, yes, I forgive you ... even though there is nothing you have done that needs forgiving!"

Still kneeling, the brothers embraced for a long time, while Tychicus and Apphie stood as tear-filled witnesses to this miraculous scene of restoration.

Right at that moment, Archie walked into the room, having heard that his brother had returned home. He walked in to see these two men that he loved dearly embracing. Without hesitation, he raced over and joined the brothers' embrace. He too became a blubbering mess for some time. As his eyes cleared ... with a wink, he encouraged Apphia and Tychicus to join in the group hug.

The celebrations of this restoration went on well into the night and the next day. At the dinner table that evening Philemon announced to those present that Onesimus was now a freed slave. He proudly presented him with his manumission documents (certificate of freedom). He was also offered to live in the oikos, having his own bedroom chamber, if he would like.

As a *libertinus* (freed slave), he was of course, free to leave if he chose to. Onny looked at both his brothers — his gaze shifting from one to the other for some time. It was not that he was searching for an answer to Philemon's proposal; he was simply searching their faces for reassurance.

✍

Contemplations for Individual Reflection and Group Discussion

CHAPTERS #26 - #27:

- Consider Proverbs 3:5-6. Read it in different versions. Make some notes about: How? What? When? Why? Who?

- Have you ever returned to the place — especially the house or street — where you grew up? How did it feel?

- Remember the first personal letter you received. Who sent it and what was their reason for sending it?

- Has there ever been a time when you have to confess something to someone close to you? How was it received?

- Have you ever experienced or been involved in the restoration of a broken relationship? What was that like emotionally?

EPILOGUE

Circa AD 60 ...

I want to begin drawing my speculations on Onesimus' incredible journey to freedom toward a feasible conclusion. In my heart of hearts, I would like to believe the best outcome for this story. Therefore, I propose the following thoughts:

Onesimus continued to grow in his faith while embracing his newfound freedom as a *libertinus*, flourishing as he assimilated into his extended family. In consultation with Philemon, Apphia, and Archippus, he was encouraged to initiate a mentoring program for young slaves in the area. He focused on positive self-affirmation, teaching basic reading and writing, and most significantly, sharing his faith in Jesus.

Philemon and Apphia remained childless, yet they took many local children under their wing through regular Gospel outreach events on their *oikos* estate. They continued pastoring the Laodicean church community, which met in their home. Their church grew in faith and numbers, benefiting from the ongoing mentoring support of the Colossian Christians.

Archippus thrived in his ministry to both slaves and masters throughout the region. As master of horses, he was a gifted teacher — also able to use his knowledge of horses to teach new disciples about obedience and rebellion. He led many to Christ and witnessed a shift in the attitudes of masters toward their slaves. Even more importantly, he helped slaves realize that their true freedom was found in Christ. He taught them to respect their masters as if they were serving the Lord Jesus himself.

This is where my speculation ceases, and I allow recorded history to take over.

Laodicea was a wealthy banking centre, proud of its abundant resources. Philemon's family business in cloth dyeing and distribution prospered as they lived out their faith through tithing and giving to the poor.

Within a year of Onesimus' return, the region suffered a massive earthquake that devastated large parts of Laodicea and Colossae. Houses, temples, businesses, and roads were reduced to rubble. The Christian community was among the first to respond, providing shelter and food to those in need.

By the providence of God, *(one final moment of speculation!)* Philemon's household, property, and business escaped significant damage from the initial earthquake — and even from subsequent aftershocks.

As word reached Rome, the government offered financial aid and labour to assist in rebuilding. However, the proud Laodiceans refused the Roman proposition, insisting that they were wealthy enough to restore their city without outside help. Rather than accepting imperial aid, they relied on their own resources, rejecting any notion of dependence or charity.

Yet, for all their wealth, Laodicea lacked something essential — water. Unlike nearby mountain towns with cold, refreshing streams or Hierapolis with its renowned hot springs, Laodicea had no natural water source. Instead, water had to be transported through aqueducts, arriving lukewarm and filled with sediment. Cold water ... we know ... is good for drinking, and hot springs are valued for their healing properties. But lukewarm, sediment-filled water neither offered refreshment nor healing. For the Laodiceans, there water supply was unpleasant and unfit for use.

Over time, this independent, self-sufficient mindset crept into the Laodicean Christian community, weakening their spiritual effectiveness. This attitude was directly addressed by Jesus Himself before the close of the first century. From the Isle of Patmos, John the Apostle recorded the Lord's rebuke in the Book of Revelation:

> 4 "Write this letter to the angel of the church in Laodicea. This is the message from the one who is the Amen—the faithful and true witness, the beginning of God's new creation:
>
> 15 "I know all the things you do, that you are neither hot nor cold. I wish that you were one or the other! 16 But since you are like lukewarm water, neither hot nor cold, I will spit you out of my mouth! 17 You say, 'I am rich. I have everything I want. I don't need a thing!' And you don't realize that you are wretched and miserable and poor and blind and naked. 18 So I advise you to buy gold from me — gold that has been purified by fire. Then you will be rich. Also buy white garments from me so you will not be shamed by your nakedness, and ointment for your eyes so you will be able to see."
>
> **New Living Translation**

Jesus tells the Laodicean church that they are just like their water supply:

"I know your works: you are neither cold nor hot. Would that you were either cold or hot! So, because you are lukewarm, and neither hot nor cold, I will spit you out of my mouth." *(Revelation 3:15–16, NIV)*

Jesus is not saying that He would prefer people to be spiritually cold rather than lukewarm. Nowhere does God desire His people to have cold hearts. Rather, He clarifies what He means in the next verse:

"For you say, I am rich, I have prospered, and I need nothing, not realizing that you are wretched, pitiable, poor, blind, and naked." *(Revelation 3:17, ESV)*

The Laodicean church believed they had everything they needed. But in reality, their spiritual self-sufficiency left them impoverished, blind, and ineffective for the kingdom of God.

In keeping with the theme of this book, one could say that the Laodicean church sadly had become *achrestos* — *USELESS* — while still remaining *euchristos* — in Christ.

TIMELINE

Speculated Timeline —

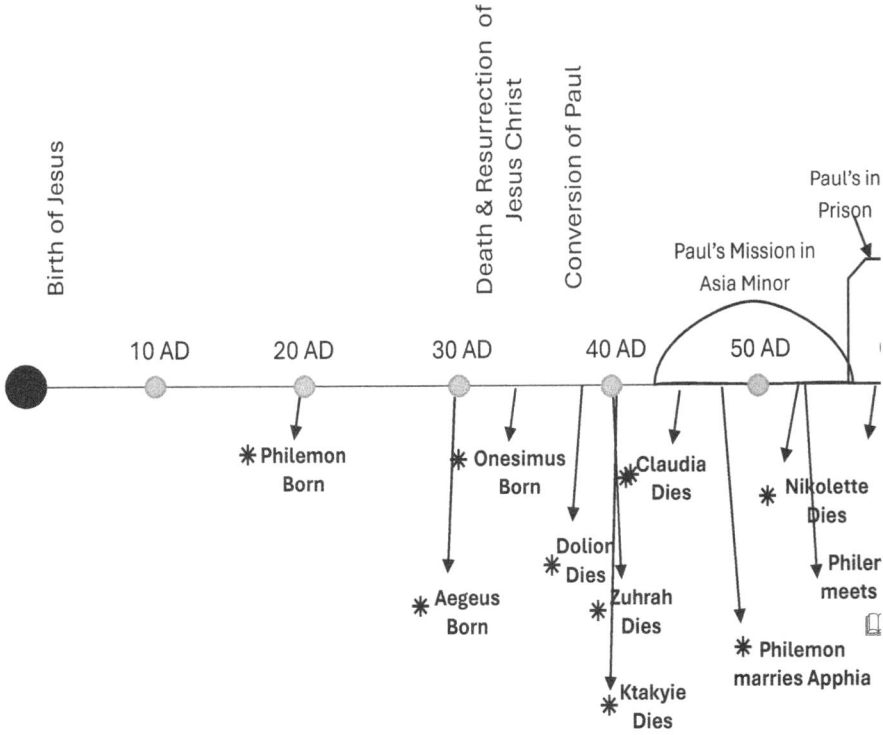

Birth of Jesus

Death & Resurrection of Jesus Christ

Conversion of Paul

Paul's Mission in Asia Minor

Paul's in Prison

10 AD 20 AD 30 AD 40 AD 50 AD

✳ Philemon Born

✳ Onesimus Born

✳ Claudia Dies

✳ Nikolette Dies

Dolion ✳ Dies

✳ Aegeus Born

Zuhrah ✳ Dies

Philer meets 📖

✳ Philemon marries Apphia

✳ Ktakyie Dies

LEGEND:
HISTORICAL / BIBLICAL ... ABOVE THE LINE
SPECULATED ... ✳ BELOW THE LINE
BIBLICAL ... 📖 BELOW THE LINE

198

— Philemon / Onesimus

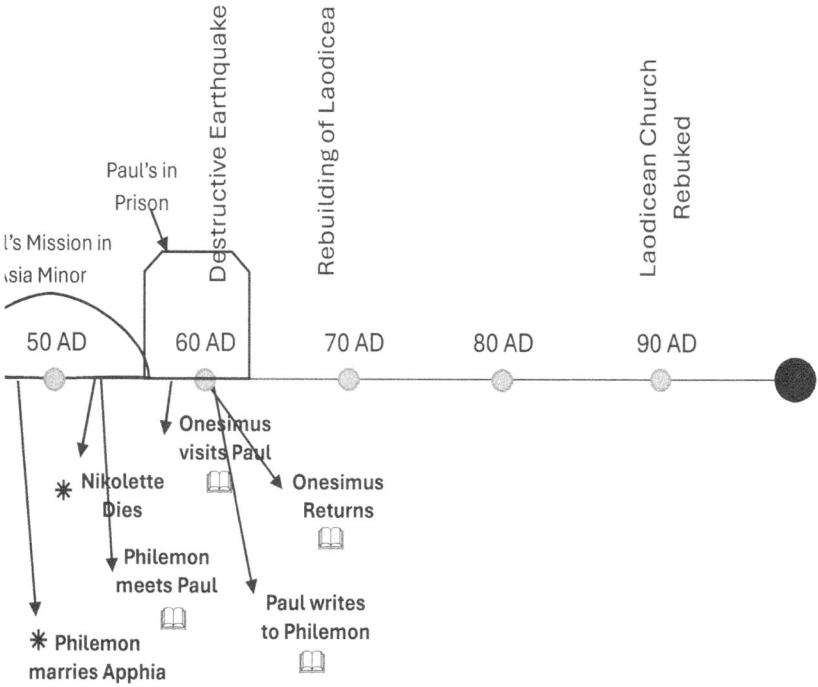

Destructive Earthquake

Rebuilding of Laodicea

Laodicean Church
Rebuked

Paul's in
Prison

l's Mission in
ısia Minor

50 AD   60 AD   70 AD   80 AD   90 AD

Onesimus
visits Paul

Nikolette
Dies

Onesimus
Returns

Philemon
meets Paul

Paul writes
to Philemon

Philemon
marries Apphia

© Gary B Lewis
2025

199

GLOSSARY OF TERMS

TERM	LANGUAGE	MEANING
adelphos	Greek	brother
patéras	Greek	father
mitéra	Greek	mother
apóstolos	Greek	sent one / apostle
oikos	Greek	house / property
stoa	Greek	lean-to /covered area
wendme	Amharic	brother
libertinus	Latin	freed slave
Emaye	Amharic	mother
Abaye	Amharic	father
manumission	Latin	documents of freedom
colossinum	Greek	red woollen cloth
doulos/douloi	Greek	slave/s
Kyrios	Greek	master
Despoina	Greek	mistress / wife of master
maieutikos	Greek	mid-wife
kommáti antístasis	Greek	cherry on the top
prothesis	Greek	laying out of a dead body
ekphora	Greek	funeral procession
peculium	Greek	payment to slaves
andron	Greek	an apartment for men
Onyame	Amharic	God

OTHER BOOKS

by
Gary Lewis

HE TOOK MY LUNCH* - A Miracle through the Eyes of a Boy [adults/teens]

VERTICALLY CHALLENGED* - The Ups and Downs of Praying [adults/teens]

PRAYER BUBBLES* - Turning Thoughts into Prayers for Prayer Hesitants [adults/teens]

AN EPISTLE TO AN APOSTLE* - Titus writes to Paul (a novella Bible story) [adults/teens]

LITTLE BOY ALL LOCKED UP* (a novella about anger, grief & loss) [all ages]

STOLEN TRUTH AND THE DARK-HOODED THIEF* (a novella about lying & stealing) [all ages]

JESSICA FINDS TRUE VALUE (a picture story book about self-worth) [10 years +]

JACKSON'S HIDDEN TREASURE (a picture story book about self-worth) [10 years +]

OLIVIA'S JAR OF PICKLED INSPIRATION (a picture story book about positive affirmation) [10 years +]

* specific Christian content

www.gablesbooks.com

ABOUT the AUTHOR

Gary Lewis is a retired Primary School Chaplain and mentor to School Chaplains. His background has involved Primary School education, Children's Ministry including Church Pastor. His extensive lay ministry covering more than 50 years, has also involved Worship Leading, Preaching, Prayer Ministry Coordinator and Church leadership.

He has been married to Maree for more than 50 years, with 3 children and 7 grandchildren. In his retirement, Gary continues mentoring in various capacities, as well as running several workshops in different fields ... including prayer, discipleship, writing and storytelling.

-

www.ingramcontent.com/pod-product-compliance
Ingram Content Group UK Ltd.
Pitfield, Milton Keynes, MK11 3LW, UK
UKHW022033310325
456929UK00007B/650

"I'm not useless!" Who said that?

The subtitle of this book provides the answer: "I Am Onesimus."

But who was Onesimus, and why would anyone consider him useless in the first place? What led him to declare, "I'm not useless"?

In this compelling story, author Gary Lewis creates a backstory that sheds light on who the biblical character Onesimus was. Where and when he lived. And why he was a slave in the first-place.

In this book, you will follow Onesimus's transformative journey from slavery to faith in Jesus Christ.

From beginning to the end, the reader will be kept wondering if he will ever gain his freedom.

ISBN 978-0-6455552-9-5

9 780645 555295